Christmas 2021

Dear Judy,

Merry Christmas to
a friend for nearly 60
years! I hope this book
brings back some fun
memories of our time
together at good ol' PHS!

Love,
Trixie

# You're Welcome, Purdy High!

WACKY TALES FROM A SMALL-TOWN
HIGH SCHOOL GIRL IN THE EARLY SIXTIES

## TRIXIE POOR

LifeRich Publishing is a registered trademark of
The Reader's Digest Association, Inc.

LifeRich Publishing books may be ordered
through booksellers or by contacting:

LifeRich Publishing
1663 Liberty Drive
Bloomington, IN 47403
www.liferichpublishing.com
1 (888) 238-8637

Keywords:
Humorous; Fiction; Adventures; Short Stories;
High School; Sixties; Small-town

ISBN: 978-1-4897-1155-7 (sc)
ISBN: 978-1-4897-1154-0 (e)

Library of Congress Control Number: 2017902326

Print information available on the last page.

LifeRich Publishing rev. date: 03/09/2017

For Cody,
the hot air in my balloon.
with all my love

# CONTENTS

# ACKNOWLEDGMENTS

My utmost gratitude to John Nelson, a brilliant writer and friend for over fifty years, who edited this book for me. Besides making sure I didn't get too carried away with commas, John gave me the confidence to keep writing.

A huge thank you to Waldinei Lafaiete of Lafaiete Photography in Helotes, Texas, who generously offered his time and expertise to provide me with the author photo.

And my deepest thanks to family - especially my son, Dr. Sean E. Garcia - and friends who encouraged me to turn my stories into a book. As Trixie Poor from Purdy would say, "You know who you are!"

# INTRODUCTION

This book is for anyone seeking a laugh-out-loud read. Through hilariously funny, far-fetched escapades, a teenage girl recounts her high school years while, at the same time, revealing small-town life in the early Sixties. A delightfully wacky and engaging romp back in time!

# PERILS OF PAINTING THE "P"

Once upon a time, many long years ago, there was a mountain that afforded a spectacular view of the surrounding area. A few settlers happened upon this mountain, looked out onto the land below, and thought it would be a good place to begin life anew. Two of the forefathers, husky farmers named Methuselah McDonald and Hans Burger, remarked to their wiry rancher friends, Hamish Wealthley and Patrick Banks, "Ain't that a purdy sight?" Mr. Wealthley and Mr. Banks agreed, as did the rest of the pioneers. Then one of the gold miners, Junior Rockafellow, quickly put in his two cents' worth. "Hey, I got an idea for the name of the town! How 'bout we call it 'Purdy'?" All the founders agreed and with that the town of Purdy was born. Liking the name "Purdy" very much, they all whooped and hollered and shouted "Yippee!" at the top of their lungs. And with that the county of Yippee was named ----

"Trixie! Are you paying attention? Your eyes are nearly

shut and there's drool oozing out of the corner of your mouth."

"Oh, yes, Mr. Peabody," I replied, blinking my eyes and wiping my chin. "You were telling us about . . . uh, the history of Purdy. Very interesting, I must say."

Very interesting, indeed. About as interesting as watching dust accumulate on a windowsill. Mr. Arlo Peabody, my history teacher, continued with his monotonous lecture as I tried to piece together what he'd been telling us. There'd been something about hamburgers, I think, and rich people . . . and how Purdy got its name. Oh, to be perfectly honest, I may have missed a few minor details here and there regarding names and dates. My mind was busy thinking about more important things, like the upcoming painting of the "P" on that same historical mountain Mr. Peabody was droning on about.

I'd been helping to paint the "P" ever since I was a freshman at good ol' Purdy High, a couple of years earlier, in 1961. Every October the Purdy High School Student Council and the Squirrelettes, the girls pep club, were in charge of whitewashing the "P" ---- a giant white letter that could be seen from everywhere in Purdy. Our school mascot was the squirrel, which meant it was a protected species in Yippee County. Housewives could no longer bag a squirrel for Sunday dinner, thereby saving themselves two bits. All the ladies were forced to buy their meat at the Dandy Food Basket. I'm not sure who decided on a squirrel for the mascot, but it must have been one of the forward-thinking early settlers. Maybe it's in my history book somewhere. I'll have to ask Mr. Peabody.

The annual event was going to take place on a Saturday, which I didn't think was a very good idea. At one of the student council meetings, I'd suggested we do the project on a Friday instead. My reason for this was quite logical. Since so many of the kids went to matinees at the Moose Theater to see Dracula or Tammy and the Bachelor, I figured Saturday afternoon should be kept free. And as for the morning, well, many Purdy Squirrel girls washed their hair at that time, and the Squirrel boys had to mow lawns. Plus, and this had absolutely nothing at all to do with my argument, there was a geometry test scheduled for that Friday. I tried my best to convince the council, the pep club and the administration that Friday was definitely a better day for the whitewash project, but my ingenious proposal was shot down by every one of those closed-minded ninnies!

The other swell idea I had was to paint the letter a vibrant glow-in-the-dark orange. Such a dramatic improvement would make our "P" stand out from all the other mountain letters around the state. And if we received several inches of snow in the winter, as was often the case, we'd be able to see our "P" a whole lot easier. Once again, sadly, my input got booed by those narrow-minded squares. It was becoming increasingly difficult to be so far ahead of one's own time.

Reverting back to the boring ol' ways, one sunny,

Saturday morning the Purdy Squirrels, who wanted to help slap paint on the "P," met in the PHS parking lot to be driven over to the base of the mountain. A lot of the boys had pickups, mostly borrowed from dads or older brothers, and the rest of us were able to pile into the backs willy-nilly ---- legs, arms, heads, whatever, dangling off the sides. Most of the drivers stayed within the speed limit but if a teacher weren't along, certain maniacs would charge lickety-split around Purdy until we were finally, literally, dumped at our destination. Forming a human chain to carry the bags of whitewash, buckets of water, brushes and other necessary tools to the top, the kids completed the back-breaking chore in under an hour. I, myself, was not part of the actual chain, but rather the self-appointed supervisor who made sure there were no breaks in the chain. I walked alongside the line, sipping water from a paper cup and fanning myself with my empty Frito bag ---- essentially making sure that every loyal Purdy Squirrel was doing his or her fair share. Once at the top, we were ready to begin the fun part!

I wasn't technically in charge, but when I witnessed some terrible goofs being perpetrated against the glorious "P" I had to step in! A few go-getters, mainly Hubert Button, Ralphie Tittsworth, and Clarence Waddle, were so enthusiastic about their responsibility that they were in the process of sloshing whitewash to form another hump! This oversight meant the "P" was turning into a big, fat "B"! I was absolutely horrified! Can you imagine the repercussions if I'd allowed this to happen? Visitors would think they were in some weird town named Burdy; peppy cheerleaders would chant Go Burdy Squirrels, Go!; the prestigious town paper would be called The Burdy Evening Courier. Honestly, it's a good thing I caught that one in time!

But at least those three goofballs were working, if you could call it that. Several of the guys were . . . uh . . . how can I put this nicely . . . lollygagging! There, I said it! When I noticed them stretched out on a patch of wildflowers with their hands entwined behind their necks and their eyes closed, I quickly grabbed a whitewash stirrer and started poking them in the ribs to wake them up. What made me really mad was the fact that they were lying upon yellow daisies, my favorite flower! Davey Goodnuff, one of the worst offenders, jumped up and began reaching for my neck. Any other time I wouldn't have minded but I thought kissing me now, in front of all these other kids, not to mention the teachers, was highly inappropriate.

"Knock it off, Davey!" I scolded. "If you want a kiss you'll have to take me on a proper date! I've never been on one before, but I've heard stories from my friends. We could go to the Purdy Bowling Lanes or you could buy me a cheeseburger at the Gulp n Gobble. Margie and Bonita tell me their boyfriends take them to the Saturday afternoon matinees and get them munchies like popcorn and Milk Duds. What would you like to do?"

Davey got this strange look on his face like I was

speaking Swahili, then he lowered his arms and said, "Trixie, you're the biggest nut in the school!" As he began slowly backing away from me, I thought to myself, "That's just like a boy. Always playing hard to get."

The only boy I didn't jab with that four-foot pole was the adorable Billy Bunson and there was a darn good reason for it. The year before, Billy had written the sweetest thing in my school yearbook, The Yippee Book. He'd put, "To the prettiest girl in our class. I'll never forget you." Wasn't that nice? It turned out he thought he was writing in Lulu Dilly's book, but oh well . . . It was in MY book and I still liked it. In fact, on those very rare occasions when I felt a trifle down in the dumps, I'd get out my yearbook and reread those lovely words.

The girls were doing okay at their job, pulling weeds and cleaning up the area surrounding the "P" letter. The only complaint I had about them was their tendency to yank out the flowers and leave the weeds. I became particularly upset when they reached for the yellow daisies. They weren't doing this intentionally, of course; they simply did not have my extensive knowledge of botany. When I tried to give them lessons about which plants to pull and which to leave, they simply stuck out their tongues and told me to get lost.

"It's not that we don't know the difference, Trixie," my best friend, Margery Sweetum, had confided. "It's that we can't gawk at the boys and pull weeds at the same time." And with that admission of guilt, Margery or Margie, as I called her when I was in a hurry, retrieved a tube of ChapStick from her jeans pocket and began slathering her lips, making her kisser look like a couple of white birthday candles.

In the midst of all this chaos, there was Barney Flume, the self-appointed school photographer. The dad of the 6'5", 120-pound Barney owned the Purdy Camera Mart so Barney had access to all the film and flash bulbs he wanted. He labeled himself a "free lance photographer" but most of us just labeled him a dopey kid who was always in the way. He was wandering around, camera dangling from his scrawny neck, stepping on all the pretty, yellow daisies, until I yelled at him to get out of the way and go take a picture of a rock or something.

With the kids somewhat under control and Barney off taking pictures of boulders, I turned my attention to the teachers. Every single PHS teacher that I'd ever had a class with was crazy about me, as well as most who hadn't had the delight of seeing my smiling face in their classroom. I don't recall them using those exact words ---- "We're crazy about you, Trixie" ---- however, I do remember the word "crazy" being flung about somewhere in our conversations. Pop McNultie, the geometry teacher, was doing his part to spruce up the side of the hill as was Mr. Bunson, the biology teacher whose son, Billy, wrote that tribute to me in The Yippee Book. Also lending a hand was Coach Cole Goodman. Coach Goodman was a P.E. teacher, drivers education instructor, head baseball coach, football coach, basketball coach, and powderpuff football coach.

And he had a wife and a little redheaded, freckle-faced whippersnapper named Corky, who was my babysitting charge. In Coach's spare time he volunteered for neat stuff such as the all-important painting of the "P."

I decided it would be a nice gesture on my part to thank these old folks for helping out. When I finished my thank-you speech, they all smiled lamely. Then Mr. Bunson offered, "Actually, Trixie, at the last faculty meeting we were the ones who picked the short straws."

I didn't really know what picking straws had to do with anything, so I just nodded like I knew exactly what he was talking about; I was very good at doing that.

Finally, after laboring under the sweltering sun for what seemed like five days, but was really only five hours according to my Timex, teachers and students alike took a lunch break and were asked by Mr. Fuffenhoff, the PHS principal, to line up. The kids were queuing up nicely, but the teachers were in a big clump around the soda pops, thereby monopolizing said drinks.

Well, I knew the teachers were in charge during the week, but this was Saturday. Why should they be in charge of me on a Saturday? Wasn't Monday through Friday good enough for them? I approached the group of geezers, cleared my throat, then started in. "Excuse me, but you're creating quite a bottleneck here. Some of the rest of us would like a Coke, too. I think you need to spread out and let some of the people who did most of the work, like me, get in here and -----"

"Trixie Poor! Just who do you think you are?" barked Mr. Nikniewicz, the journalism teacher.

I wanted to reply, "I'm Trixie Poor. You just said my name so why are you asking?" but since I sometimes knew when to shut my trap, I just stood there until Mr. Nick was done yammering away.

"If you don't stop being so bossy, I'll make sure you never work on The Squirrely Times school paper or The Yippee Book. I've never seen a kid as bossy as you!"

Goodness. The only thing I could think of that would make him get so worked up and spout off such nonsense was the blistering heat. I wanted to comply with his tirade, but it wouldn't be easy since I didn't even know what I'd been bossy about. I was merely stating the obvious. But rather than get Mr. Nikniewicz frothing at the mouth again, I clamped my mouth shut, after meekly replying, "Yes, sir."

I really had no choice but to close my pie hole, as I had every intention of being an editor on The Squirrely Times. I firmly believed that natural writing talents such as mine ---- and Tolstoy's ---- should never be restrained. And so far as the Yippee Book went, well . . . what's the easiest way to make sure your mug is in it a lot? Be on the staff! So I resolved to curb my "bossiness" ---- at least around Mr. Nick.

After everyone had pigged out on the lunch of hotdogs, beans, potato chips, and pop, the various committees began packing up their supplies and heading back down the mountain. Again, I felt I could serve best in a supervisory position, so I enthusiastically pointed out what needed to be done. "Don't forget that shovel, Ralphie! You missed that rake over by that rock, Hubert!" You know, helpful little tidbits like that. I won't bother to tell you what they said back to me. Humph! When we were at last packed up in our different pickups and driven back to the school parking lot, I was completely exhausted, as anyone can imagine, but very gratified to realize what an outstanding accomplishment I'd achieved.

A week later, The Squirrely Times came out with an article about Saturday's undertaking. I wasn't asked to write the article, so it wasn't very good. For one thing, there was no mention of me whatsoever. All the credit for a job well done was given to the PHS Student Council and the Purdy Squirrelettes pep club and those faculty members who "unselfishly" gave up their Saturday mornings to help. Well, what about me? I unselfishly gave up my Saturday morning to go up that mountain rather than stay home to bathe and brush my beautiful German Shepherd, Queenie. Oh well . . . I had resolved long ago to always give myself credit when others ignorantly wouldn't. Every evening, as the sun set over my peaceful hometown and I gazed upon the wondrous "P" Mountain, I was filled with the recognition that Purdy High School would never be forgotten, thanks to my supreme efforts. My eyes glistening with tears, and hugging Queenie, I whispered, "You're welcome, Purdy High!"

# ARCHERY CHAMP CHALLENGE

My favorite class at good ol' PHS was physical education. In fact, I'm pretty sure I could easily have become valedictorian of the great 1965 Class of Purdy High, had I been allowed to take only P.E. classes all four years. Unfortunately, I was forced to take many other less worthwhile subjects such as math, science and English, thereby causing a perfect straight A average to become . . . well . . . less than perfect. I excelled in all the strenuous sports, such as ping pong and badminton, but the one I was really good at was archery.

Gloating does not become me, however it must be noted that I was a loyal member of the prestigious organization, the Girls' Athletic Association, or GAA for lazy-talking people. I took part in various club-sponsored tournaments and always received recognition for being a participant. One only has to turn to page forty-six of The Yippee Book, the school yearbook, to see how active I was! The only reason I was never elected President of GAA was that Dottie Darlin, the girl whose dad owned the Purdy Bowling Lanes, offered to give a free game of bowling to anyone who voted for HER. The best I could do was offer part of my Snickers candy bar or Fritos, if preferred, during lunchtime. I lost the presidency every time due to Dottie's unscrupulous ways.

Another reason I liked P.E. so much was that we got to wear snazzy, blue, gym clothes. They were one-piece outfits that resembled jumpsuits, only with shorts, and much cuter. Every day we'd change into these little numbers for P.E. class then, at the end of class, we'd stuff them back into our P.E. locker, hoping they wouldn't get too wrinkled from all the sweat. We were supposed to take them home every Friday to be washed and then bring them back on Monday all clean and fresh, but sometimes that didn't happen. On Mondays, during roll call, Miss Corey would ask us if we'd washed our outfit over the weekend. I was always relieved to learn that every girl had although, judging by the pervasive gross smells in our locker room, I doubted if everyone had told the truth. Also, one time I "accidentally" smudged Dottie Darlin's collar with a piece of my Snickers bar and six weeks later the chocolate was still there.

One glorious day Miss Corey informed us that we were done with basketball. Good! There'd been way too much running and sweating for my liking. Instead we were going to learn the difficult, yet wonderful, skill of archery. I, personally, was thrilled beyond words! I'd been developing my archery skills since fifth grade, at which time I'd received a little bow and arrow set for Christmas from my favorite uncle, Uncle Chester. I figured I was unbeatable, having shot arrows into the pine tree on the side of our house on many occasions. One time I missed the tree and hit the kitchen window instead, which caused my mom to overreact. But that was just once and my mom had been a good two inches away from where the arrow hit. However, Kitty Shrub, my friend since junior high, bragged that one of her uncles, who went by the unattractive (in my opinion) name of Otis, was a competitive archer and had taught her everything he knew. Humph!

"So you think you're better than me, huh, Kitty? Well, let's just see about that. How 'bout we have a little contest, just the two of us, to find out who the better archer is!"

"Oh, you don't scare me, Trixie. I'll gladly compete with you. Uncle Otis says I'm the best he's ever seen for a girl my age."

How unseemly. All that boasting. You'd never catch me talking like that.

"Well, Kitty Cat, my uncle Chester who's a plumber ---- and a darn good one at that ----says I'm the best he's ever seen for a girl my age. And he's the one who gave me that bow and arrow set for Christmas, so he ought to know! Not only that, but Uncle Chester can wiggle his ears. Can you wiggle your ears, Kitty? I can! I stand in front of the mirror practicing, but the only way I can get them to wiggle is to keep my emerald green eyes closed good and tight, so

I never actually see them wiggling. I can just tell by the way the inside of my head feels. Can you do that, Kitty?"

Kitty refused to acknowledge when she'd been beaten. Her stubbornness was turning into a very undesirable quality. "Trixie, since you seem to think you're as good an archer as me, even though I always hit the tiny center circle, whereas you can't hit any part of the target, let alone the bullseye, let's do this. Let's each get one of our friends to put an apple on her head and we can shoot it off, just like William Tell. You do know who William Tell is, don't you, Trixie?"

"Yes, I know who William Tell is, Kitty. Any nitwit knows William Tell invented the bow and arrow so he could steal from the rich and give to the poor! Now, who wants to be my helper?" Several girls scattered behind the trees bordering McNultie Field, the area where we were honing our archery skills.

Since Miss Corey always took her own sweet time showing up to the field, I made a suggestion to Kitty. "Tomorrow, bring your apple and your helper. If we hurry, we'll be finished with the contest before Miss Blue Hair shows up." Kitty thought that was a swell idea and asked the class if anyone would like to be her assistant. Lots of hands shot up. When I asked the same question, not one single hand was raised. Not one single hand. I was trying to piece the mystery together when it finally hit me. Kitty was bribing them all with something! Just like Dottie Darlin! I didn't know what she had up her sleeve, but I'd get to it eventually. In the meantime, I needed somebody to be my assistant. All the girls were trying to look away from me or study something on the ground, but then I spotted one girl, trying to slink behind Kitty, who owed me a huge favor. I'd caught her cheating on a midterm geometry test, but never ratted her out. I'd noticed she'd written some answers on the palm of her left hand when I'd innocently peeked over her shoulder to copy what she'd written down for the last ten answers. Tapping her on the shoulder, I'd pointed to her hand then whispered, "You owe me." Now, a couple of weeks later, I approached the little cheater.

"So . . . remember the geometry test? Now it's time to pay the piper, so to speak." I did my best to sound menacing, since she looked as if she might put up a struggle. "Remember our deal? I don't rat you out and you help me out?"

"I know, Trixie," she acknowledged, "but isn't there something else I could do for you that wouldn't splatter me to kingdom come? Just name it! Anything!"

"Look, missy, there's nothing else I want. And where did you get this ridiculous notion that you'll be splattered? All I'm going to do is shoot a little fruit off the top of your head with an arrow. It's not like I'll be using a gun or anything . . ."

She began sniveling for no good reason. "I know all that, Trixie, but I've seen you with that bow and arrow. No offense, but you're not the best archer in the class. In fact, you're lousy. In fact, I think you're probably the worst archer in the class, if Miss Corey's opinion counts for anything, so what else ----"

"Oh, stop whining! I've got lots of time to practice before tomorrow. Would it make you feel any better if I promise to spend a good fifteen minutes shooting arrows at my pine tree today after school?"

Wiping her snotty nose on her sleeve, she hiccuped a couple of times. "I guess so. Fifteen minutes? You promise?"

"Yes, I promise. Now, is there anything else I can do for you to ease your overworked mind?" She was indeed becoming difficult.

"Well, there is one thing, Trixie. Could you not let it get around school that I'm the one helping you with this? I would hate to go down in the annals of Purdy High as 'The Stupid Idiot' who didn't have the sense of a turnip. Could you maybe just refer to me using initials? How about S.I.?"

"Of course, S.I.!" Never let it be said that I'm not a very compassionate person!

The next day, before class, the field was crowded with enthusiastic spectators. Word had spread throughout the school about our contest. Glaring at one another, Kitty and I brought forth our targets: a shiny Red Delicious for Kitty and a dull Idaho Russet for me. My mom was out of apples. Kitty's helper was Sugar Wiggins, who I'd always thought of as one of my best friends, but now I considered a treacherous fiend! I scowled at Sugar and furrowed my brow with all my might. Sensing my displeasure, my fair-weather friend tried to explain away her betrayal, "Sorry,

Trixie, I'd like to help you out, but I really would like to live long enough to graduate with the class." Oh, who needed Sugar anyway? I had S.I.

"Okay, Kitty, since you won the coin toss, you can go first," I generously offered, displaying my usual sportsmanship. Sportsmanship. Now there's a word for an award the school should start handing out. I could win that one hands down. As soon as I had a minute I was going to take a little detour to Mr. Fuffenhoff's office and see about starting that award. Or maybe Mr. Rizzo's office. No, definitely not Mr. Rizzo's office. Mrs. Snotgrass, my French teacher, might be lurking about. Yes, the principal's office, not the assistant principal's. Yep, sportsmanship award . . .

Anyway, Kitty and Sugar took their places on the field and Sugar carefully balanced the apple on top of her bouffant hairdo. I ever so kindly suggested to Sugar that she might want to remove the blue bow that was bobby pinned between the bangs and the poofy part as it constituted, in my expert opinion, a major hindrance. Sugar merely crossed her eyes, poked her thumbs in her ears and began waggling them, then stuck her tongue out at me. Meanwhile Kitty, with all the self-assurance of an Olympic athlete, took careful aim at the target and let the arrow fly! The apple was hit directly in the center, making for a perfect shot, or so proclaimed all those who were watching. I, on the other hand, determined it could have been a little more to the right. Nevertheless, the entire crowd began cheering wildly. Sugar reached up and removed the squishy fruit from her noggin, then demurely took a little curtsy. Kitty, quite haughtily I thought, started bowing in all directions. Oh, for pity's sake! I tossed my chin and ordered S.I. to go stand on her spot.

Right away I felt at a huge disadvantage. How is any normal person, no matter how tremendously gifted and capable, supposed to hit a small target like a medium-sized potato when the head it's sitting on is trembling like a sapling in a windstorm? Or when the head it's sitting on is crying uncontrollably? Believe me, I was having a heck of a time concentrating with all that shaking, rattling and rolling going on.

"Stop moving around, S.I.!" I bellowed, trying not to show exasperation at her unlimited thoughtlessness. "Do you have any idea how hard you're making this for me?" More selfish sobbing and wiggling from my incompetent helper.

Well, I couldn't wait all day. S.I. was showing no signs of getting control of herself in the foreseeable future, so I pulled the bowstring and arrow back, took aim at the target and then . . . out of nowhere . . . I heard a piercing, "Nooo ---- !" The shriek startled me so fiercely it caused me to raise my bow, launch the wayward arrow and hit a low-flying crow smack dab in the rear end!

"What on earth?!" I yelled. "Who's the nincompoop who hollered at me like that? Don't you know you should never, ever, under any circumstances . . . oh, hi, Miss

Corey," I mumbled, gazing down at a skinny, little, crumpled up ball on the ground. "Sorry about the bird. I'm afraid it's a prime example of being in the wrong place at the wrong time."

Miss Corey continued to hyperventilate, fading in and out of consciousness, until Mrs. Shott, the school nurse, arrived on the scene and placed a cool, damp rag on her brow. Miss Corey didn't return to school for several weeks after that, stating she had no recollection of what had happened that day. Come to think of it, I believe she returned the exact same day I was put in drivers ed with Coach Goodman. It was too bad I hadn't had an opportunity to tell her I'd forgiven her for messing up my chance to be the archery champ and for making me hit that crow. By the way, in case you're a bird lover, the careless fowl made a full recovery, except for the slight wobble when he flew too fast. And what happened to S.I.? She disappeared for several days, along with my vegetable. Various sources told me her mother was pretty steamed, so I made myself scarce whenever I got wind of the old gal being around my neck of the woods. I'm still alive and kicking, so it's safe to assume she never caught up with me.

Every chance she got, Kitty continued to declare herself archery champ. The Squirrely Times even wrote a front-page article about "Kitty Shrub and her amazing prowess in the sport of archery." Well, she may have gotten her picture in the school paper, along with that dumb, overstated article, but before you make any decisions about who truly deserves the title of PHS Archery Champ ---- me or Kitty ---- just ask yourself this one very important question: How many birds did KITTY get?!

# HOMECOMING GAME GLORY

I had many accomplishments during my high school years in the early Sixties, but winning Purdy High's first homecoming game since 1955 was one of the first and greatest! Purdy High could rarely manage a football win and had a previous twenty-two-game losing streak to prove it. Nobody in Purdy blamed the boys; they were just as athletic as any other guys in the state, probably even more so. Many lived on farms or ranches, making them stronger and more resilient than most of the city slickers, especially those found in Furnace City. The fault for the continual losses lay, quite simply, with the coaching staff. We were all aware of that fact, but it had been hard to find a decent head football coach who wanted to move to a little town that was beautiful, yet decidedly off-the-beaten-track. Hope was all but lost until Mr. Oliver arrived from who-knows-where. He was our light at the end of the tunnel.

We lost the first six games of the 1961 season. As if that

weren't bad enough, in some of those games we hadn't scored a single point. It was a crying shame, but all due to the obstinacy of the coaching staff. Coach Oliver, along with the assistant coaches/teachers, steadfastly refused to allow me into the locker room, or to permit me to participate in the brainstorming sessions with the players. Those old coots even refused me access to the playbook, stating some gibberish about me having "no knowledge whatsoever" about the sport of football. It was true that watching most parts of the game made about as much sense to me as observing a pile of scurrying ants in a raked-over ant hill, but those stubborn geezers forgot I'd been in charge of the towels for the Powder Puff game! I tried reminding them about that every chance I got, often stopping them in between classes, but it didn't matter. They continued to shut me out and the boys continued to lose.

At long last the biggest game of the season, the PHS Homecoming Game, was upon us. All of Purdy had geared up for the event. Storefronts of family-owned businesses were plastered with pep posters. Homeroom floats were constructed out of chicken wire stuffed with pastel-colored toilet paper and strewn with crepe paper. They were then paraded around the Yippee County Courthouse Plaza, before making their way to the Purdy Football Field. KNUT 97.3, the local radio station, was set up to broadcast the long-anticipated game. Everyone within earshot of Purdy was ready to take on the Central High team from the big metropolis of Furnace City. That evening the Purdy Football Field, where the action was to take place, was electric with excitement.

My two best friends, Margery Sweetum and Bonita Ruiz, and I made our way up the bleachers to the girls' rooting section. Since our school mascot was the squirrel, the obvious name for the girls' pep club was the Squirrelettes. Naturally we sat with our fellow Squirrelettes in order to cheer on all the boys we had crushes on, which was every single one, if I recall correctly ---- which I do, because I have an outstanding memory. Margie and Bonita were sweet kids but they knew nothing about football, unlike yours truly who'd gained considerable expertise doing that towel thing. I knew the girls always wanted to sit next to me so I could explain what was going on.

"Okay, girls, listen up. Let me give you a rundown on football. Football is a weird combination of many sports: baseball, track, and soccer. You can throw the ball to your teammates, like you do in baseball, but they never throw it back, so where's the fun in that? Sometimes the boys line up like they're going to run a track race, but the guys on the other team do the same thing, so they all end up running into each other. Finally, you can kick the ball like you're playing soccer, but I don't recommend this because someone on the other team always catches it and runs right at you knocking you down, if you don't get out of the way fast enough. That's about all there is to football. Any questions?"

"I have a question, Trixie. Don't you think Dickie Darlin looks swell in his football uniform?" asked Margie.

"Oh, good grief, Margie. What kind of question is that? Of course he looks fabulous in his football outfit. Now, are you happy? How many years have you been carrying a torch for that guy?" She refused to answer, so I pressed on, "Now, do you have a real question or are you perfectly clear on how the game of football is played?"

"Perfectly clear, Trixie, thanks to your EXCELLENT explanation." She and Bonita looked at each other, then looked away quickly, but not before I noticed some serious eye-rolling going on between them. "And here's something else you should know," I persisted. "See those big signs that have numbers on them down at the end of the field? Well, we're the home team and Central High is the visitors." Bonita rolled her program into a cone and bopped me over the head with it.

The first part of the game moved right along. They scored . . . we scored . . . we scored . . . they scored . . . blah, blah, so as intermission was approaching the score was tied, with our boys on the ten-yard line. I cleverly deduced that this would be the perfect time to make a beeline for the Booster Club Snack Bar. I really needed a Coke after all that yelling ---- about what, I wasn't sure ---- and figured I'd be the only one in line if I went right then, before the intermission show. Turns out I was right! I was the only one there, although I did have to wait to get my pop since the two people taking my order had to watch something happening on the field. They cheered, so I guess it was good. Anyway, with time to spare, I made it back to my seat for the intermission performances. My favorite part of the game!

Onto the field strutted the band, preceded by the pom-pom girls. They performed so wonderfully that I thought it would be a really neat idea to forget the rest of that boring football game and watch the band and the girls instead. I knew that I, personally, could watch their show at least five or six more hours and I was quite sure everyone else would agree with me.

Grabbing my megaphone, I hollered into it as loud as my lungs would let me, "Hey, everybody! Who'd like to forget the rest of this silly game and stick with the band and pom-pom girls instead?" I was so excited! I just knew I'd come up with the best idea since Purdy got its name.

"Sit down and shut up, you ninny! Can't you see we're ahead?" yelled Lulu Dilly, a girl I'd known since third grade. "What a goofy idea!" added Kitty Shrub, another good friend, but sometimes not very smart. "What are you? Some kinda nut?" shouted a whole bunch of older people I didn't even know. And with that, ninety-nine percent of the selfish people in the stands began throwing their hot dogs at me and pelting me with buttered popcorn, all the while using that word "nut" over and over!

Well, since it looked like my brilliant suggestion was falling on mean, deaf ears, I reluctantly sat back down. Actually, Margie and Bonita rather rudely SAT me down, telling me to clam up before I "mortified" them even more! Mortified?! Humph! Just see if I talk through the whole second part explaining the plays to them! Being temporarily chastised, I quietly began picking off the many kernels of popcorn that had been thrown at my blue PHS sweater and carefully popping them in my mouth. They weren't half bad, if you overlooked the occasional wool pile. Plus it saved me from having to spend one of my hard-earned dimes that I got from working at La Belle Beauty Shop.

I guess, to make the story completely factual, I should go ahead and mention the fact that homecoming royalty was presented during the intermission. These oh-so special ladies and gents were riding around the field in convertible cars, grinning from ear to ear, and waving to the crowd. The girls were wearing flimsy formal gowns and the boys were in suits. I felt kind of sorry for the girls because it was quite chilly, but not enough to offer them my PHS sweater. Since I hadn't even been considered to be part of that prestigious ceremony, I paid no further attention. Don't bother asking who those very important kids were because I don't remember, and even if I did remember, I wouldn't tell because, in my opinion, they already received enough glory.

"Trixie, stop chomping on that sweater-popcorn and pay attention to the game! We just made another touchdown!" squealed Margie. "Look! Dickie's getting ready to kick the ball for the extra point!"

I scanned the field to see if I could figure out what she was talking about, but all I could see was Barney Flume, the photographer for The Squirrely Times, our school paper, standing on the other side of the goal post, right in front of Dickey. Barney was attempting to stick a flashbulb in his camera. Dickie was heading for the football, ready to kick, when Barney flashed his camera and temporarily blinded poor Dickie. Dickie completely missed the ball as his right leg flew up at a 180-degree angle, causing him to fall flat on his bottom! The Purdy fans were outraged! Barney, who wasn't the smartest bulb in his flashbulb case, at least had the good sense to know when to run. He grabbed his gear and fled toward the street behind the field, racing at full throttle. Barney disappeared into the night, leaving cries of "Get him!" in his wake.

The game resumed with our Purdy Squirrels ahead for once, thanks to the two previous touchdowns, both of which I'd missed on account of those other more pressing things that needed tending to, like buying my pop at the snack bar. But then, as usually happens, the other team made a couple of touchdowns. Luckily for us, Central High also missed that free kick, so now the teams were once again tied. Since I was getting a trifle bored, I thought about bringing up my idea of having the band and pom-pom girls perform instead, but after what happened the last time, I thought better of it. But then, in the blink of an eye, we were no longer tied. Central had kicked something called a field goal, putting them ahead by three points.

Now we were losing and there wasn't much time left in the game. Good time to go get a Snickers candy bar.

Down I trotted to the Booster Club Snack Bar again, only this time there were quite a few people in line, including several Central High fans. A couple of them were off to the side, drinking soda pops, and jabbering about the game. I decided, for once in my life, to close my mouth and open my ears. I listened carefully, pretending to look through my purse for something, then heard one of the hefty men say, "Ever since our left tackle hurt his ankle, he can't run worth a darn. I sure hope Purdy doesn't try to run the ball up his side." His buddy replied, "All I can say is Purdy better keep passing the ball. If they decide to run it, we're in trouble." The first guy nodded and off they went to finish their drinks and watch the rest of the game.

Back in my seat, Snickers bar in hand, I gazed upon the field. Discouraged faces everywhere from the Purdy side ---- players, coaches, spectators. Well, I couldn't stand it! I knew I had to do something! I hadn't been the towel girl for the Powder Puff team for nothing and I hadn't overheard that conversation for nothing!

"Hold my snacks, girls," I instructed Margie and Bonita. "I heard something somewhere about running the ball, not passing it, so maybe that's what we need to do. I'm gonna head down there and tell Coach Bunson my idea!" Coach Bunson was my biology teacher and a pretty cool guy, even if he was prone to throwing chalkboard erasers at uncooperative students.

I scurried onto the field and began tugging on Mr. Bunson's PHS jacket. "Mr Bunson, I know how we can win the game," I exclaimed, while trying to catch my breath. But before I could get another word out, he interrupted me, "Trixie Poor, what are you doing here? Get off this field before you get trampled!" Then he walked off as if I'd never spoken to him.

In a large group of players I spotted another coach, a history teacher named Mr. Peabody. I thought perhaps he'd be more receptive to my suggestion. Quickly approaching the huddle, I grabbed Mr. Peabody by the arm. "Mr. Peabody, I know how we can win this game. You've got to listen to me! You should run the ball to the right side; don't pass it!"

He stared at me for a brief moment, then acknowledged, "Maybe you've got something there, kid. Let me see what Coach Oliver thinks. Now get off the field before you find yourself squashed like a bug! The game's nearly over."

Feeling as though I'd accomplished my mission, I charged back up the bleachers to join Margie, Bonita and the other Squirrelettes. "How'd it go, Trixie?" they all wanted to know. "I'll bet they told you to get lost, didn't they?"

"No, as a matter of fact, they didn't! Just you watch! They're going to run the ball, not pass it!" I forced myself to look down at the field, ignoring their smirks. As I stared at the game without blinking, not exactly comprehending what I was supposed to be looking at, from all around me

I began hearing shouts of disbelief and happiness: "We ran the ball! We didn't pass it! We won the game! We won the game!"

Wow! So that's what our players were doing down there! Our team had done exactly what I'd told them to do. They'd won the game because of ME! The first Homecoming Game since 1955! I looked around to tell anyone who would listen about my contribution and subsequent triumph, but all the fans were descending the bleachers in haste to congratulate the boys and coaches on the field. Players and coaches were being slapped on the back. Tears of joy were being shed by the Purdy ladies. The Squirrelettes, including Margie and Bonita, not to mention every girl in Purdy, were trying to hug and kiss the football players. The whole town was going crazy!

For a few minutes I remained alone on the bleachers, observing the elation on the field and smiling to myself. A part of me wanted to holler, "Hey, everybody, don't you know I was the one who set all this in motion? Sometimes snoopiness pays off! Don't I get any credit whatsoever?" But another part of me realized I'd never get the thanks I deserved and that was okay. I, Trixie Poor, knew in my heart what I'd done and, in the end, that was all that mattered to me. You're welcome, Purdy High.

# THANKSGIVING
# TURKEY TROT TRAGEDY

When I was a freshman at good ol' PHS in 1961, I had the biggest crush you could ever imagine on a kid who shall be called "Bud Smith." I'm not using his real name because I'd hate to be the cause of an acrimonious divorce, if his wife ever read this and threw him out in a jealous fit of rage. The only thing I will tell you is I was good buddies with his sister, Winnie Ragsdale. From here on out, I will simply refer to him as B.S., since I believe this will save us all a lot of turmoil, not to mention B.S.'s marriage. I must admit I did have a few other crushes in high school, such as every boy in the joint plus most of my male teachers. Even Pop McNultie, that grizzled old geometry teacher, who must have been at least ninety, possessed a certain animal magnetism.

And NO, I wasn't boy crazy! There was one guy I didn't like at all, by the name of Clarence Waddle, and for darn good reason! Clarence was my best friend's boyfriend, but one time he betrayed Bonita by smiling too many times at Lulu Dilly. Or as Bonita so eloquently put it, "Clarence quite blatantly bared his pearly whites to Lulu." Tiny Lulu was also my good friend, but not my BEST friend, so naturally my allegiance had to go with Bonita and since Clarence had stabbed Bonita in the back, then naturally I couldn't stand him anymore. Like it or not, that's how it works in high school.

But B.S. was the lucky guy I set my sights on. The highlight of every day for me was getting to say hi to B.S. as we passed each other in the hallway. Sometimes, if things were really going well for me, he'd even say hi back! That was about the only time of day I ever got to see him, because he was an older man. Yes, B.S. was a junior! A perfect specimen of almost-manhood, complete with crewcut, black horn-rimmed glasses, and a mild case of teenage acne. The latter didn't bother me, as I had my own issues with that cursed malady. Anyway, I had aspirations of us being together for the rest of our lives. I could envision it all as clear as day: lovely cottage with white picket fence interspersed with yellow daisies; fragrant red rose bushes edging the sidewalk; colorful geraniums hanging from window boxes. And the children ---- the adorable, flawless children. I, myself, was an only child, but I concluded that fifteen or twenty little scallywags would be just about right. I knew if we could say more than a daily two-letter greeting, our relationship might, at long last, have a chance to flourish and bloom, just as destiny had ordained. I read that last bit in a book somewhere; neat huh?

So, one day I got up the nerve to ask out my intended. The Thanksgiving Turkey Trot Dance was coming up and I jumped right in. Spilling out the words as fast as I could, I forged ahead: "Hi, Bud, would you like to go with me to the dance Friday night, even though we don't know each other very well, but I think it will be a lot of fun, and I know Winnie, and I know lots of kids who're going too, but we don't have to sit with them or anything, if you don't want to, but we can, if you do." I paused for a much-needed breath, then continued, "So?"

He blinked several times, quite fetching from behind those glasses, then drawled in a most pleasant response, "Oh . . . I don't know . . . maybe . . . well, I guess so . . . there doesn't seem to be anything better to do that night."

Oh my gosh, he said YES! B.S. was going to go to the dance with me and he was just as excited about it as I was! I tell you, I can't begin to describe the ecstasy I felt. It was somewhere between eating a six-scoop banana split and winning a school bowling tournament!

Alas, on the very day of Turkey Trot, one of the most terrible things in the world happened! I got a cold! What an absolute drag! There I was ---- puking, coughing, sneezing, and blowing my nose like a foghorn ---- all this in Mrs. Snotgrass's French class. Mrs. Snotgrass, or "Snotty" as we not-so-affectionately called her, didn't like me, because she said I talked too much in class. Snotty was constantly threatening me with a trip to Mr. Rizzo's office if I didn't shut up. Mr. Rizzo, the assistant principal, one time told me I was "breaking the law" by talking out of turn. After he said that, I was no longer impressed with his administrative abilities. And it wasn't like I went out of my way to talk. I tried to clam up (I really did) but it's extremely hard to do when you know, deep down inside, that what you have to impart is so much more important and interesting than what the teacher is rambling on about. So, in a nutshell, she had it in for me.

Considering my past history with Snotty, it was no surprise when she reported me to the school nurse, just because I'd thrown up a couple of measly times on Billy Bunson. Well, maybe six to be exact, but who's counting? I mean, since I hadn't thrown up on HER and the goofball, Billy, seemed to take it all in stride, I didn't get what the big deal was. Be that as it may, that tattletale of a French teacher ---- aka The Squealer or The Rat Fink ---- was out to get me for no good reason and promptly reported me to the school nurse, Mrs. Shott.

Up until that point, I'd always thought Mrs. Shott was okay, but after what she did to me that day, I shunned her like a Texas cockroach. Upon hearing those stories from Mrs. Snotgrass about my minor symptoms, that busybody of a school nurse ---- aka The Snoop or the Buttinski ---- made me go home, claiming some rigmarole about me contaminating the rest of the school . . . blah, blah . . . health hazard . . . blah, blah. Really, if the facts were analyzed properly, it was a clear case of overreaction by an overzealous, underpaid, medical professional. Needless to say, but I'll say it anyway because I do like to talk, this didn't bode at all well for me and the Turkey Trot. Purdy High had this dumb rule, and I DO mean dumb, that if you missed school the day of a dance, you weren't allowed to attend the dance! What sense did that make? I believe it's quite possible you could have pneumonia at four o'clock in the afternoon and be okay by seven o'clock in the evening. And I'm fairly certain there must be documented cases of such occurrences somewhere. But try telling that to anyone in the school! They wouldn't even offer to do research on the subject! Humph!

Well . . . naturally I was utterly distraught, completely hysterical, and totally devastated, as any normal person would be! After school I call B.S., in between hugs with the toilet, and tried to tell him the horrible news, but I was sobbing so uncontrollably that all I could hear him mutter on his end was, "What is this? Some kind of obscene phone call?"

Gaining control of myself, I hiccupped, "Nooo, you dope! It's me, TRIXIE! I'm trying to tell you I can't take you to the dance because those birdbrains at the school won't let me! But I have an idea. You could take my best friend, Bonita, because she just broke up with Clarence. You probably heard all about it. She caught him smiling at Lulu Dilly, and more than once, when they were all eating their sack lunches together on the gym bleachers." I knew I could trust Bonita with my precious B.S.

For some inexplicable reason, B.S. seemed to perk up. "Man, that's a swell idea, Trixie! The best one you've had in a long time! I'll call her right now! Gotta go. The Three Stooges is about to come on."

The click in my ear signaled the conversation was over. Now you see why I had such a thing for him. He was a bona fide trooper, always prepared to make the best of a bad situation.

I heard later, through the very active PHS grapevine, that poor, dear B.S. did a phenomenal job of hiding his anguish at not being able to take me and having to take one of the prettiest girls in the class instead. It seems he was able to force himself to dance every single slow dance with Bonita and, for some crazy reason, would conk the other guys in the face with his elbow whenever they tried to cut in. What a sport! Selflessly trying to show my friend a good time!

Bonita also confided to me that she'd let him take her to the Gulp n Gobble for one of their twenty-five cent burger and fries specials, but only because she was starving. She hadn't been able to eat, since her breakup with Clarence. She also mentioned the fact that B.S. had offered to drive her up to Lookout Mountain for a nighttime view of the Purdy lights, but she declined, in deference to me. I didn't understand what that had to do with me and flat out told her she'd missed a great opportunity. I'd driven up there with my parents one Sunday afternoon and the view had been spectacular. Having been up there once, I figured I'd never need to go again and certainly not at night, when you couldn't even see my house, and certainly not with a boy, who more than likely smelled like onion rings.

So why am I recounting this tale? Because I feel it's my duty to impart the following valuable lesson to all young Squirrels: Even in the darkest hour, life must go on and you can often rely on B.S. to pull you through. You're welcome, Purdy High!

# MY BRUSH WITH
# JUVENILE DELINQUENCY

For the most part, I was on the straight and narrow at good ol' Purdy High ---- didn't smoke, didn't drink, didn't rob people, rarely chewed gum in class, one time talked in class ---- but this fateful afternoon in October, things went horribly awry: I cut class!

Right after scarfing down our sack lunches, which we ate while sitting on the gym bleachers, Lulu Dilly and I strolled into girls chorus EARLY. Normally I wouldn't bring up such a fact, but this deserves special mention, since it's a once-in-a-lifetime event. Settling into our assigned spots, we began looking around and noticed something was missing. Handsome Mr. Campbell, our bagpipe-playing teacher, was nowhere to be found. Usually he could be seen bustling around, arranging sheet music, giving instructions to the accompanist, and yelling at overly active kids to settle down, but the only one standing before us today was a mousy little woman wearing a terrified look on her face. At that moment, the realization hit us! We have a substitute! Four words that brought moans of ecstasy to every Purdy Squirrel.

Along with a substitute came numerous benefits, the main one being no dreaded pop quiz. Of course, this didn't matter in chorus. However, even in chorus, being "taught" by a substitute afforded us certain liberties otherwise refused to us. The only times having a sub wasn't a good thing were if said sub was your Sunday School teacher, or your next-door neighbor, or your good friend's mother, or the wife of your English teacher. Then all bets were off and you had to behave a little bit. Sadly, this happened all too often in our small town, but today we were in luck! This poor soul, quaking in front of us, was a complete unknown!

As the frightened creature before us began shuffling from side to side and looking furtively around as if seeking an escape route, Lulu leaned over and whispered in my ear, "Let's ditch."

Lulu was my alto buddy, school bus partner, and good friend, so I wondered what had come over her. Ditch! Heck, I had never in my life ditched a class! I'd overheard other kids talking about having done such an outrageous thing, but me? I was flabbergasted at the thought!

"Oh, c'mon, Trixie, you big fat chicken. Miss Scaredy Sub doesn't even know how to take roll in this class. We can slip out before she licks her pencil to start. Let's head over to the Gulp n Gobble for a cherry Coke."

Oh my gosh. I wanted to, but I was afraid. But then again, would anyone find out? No, we were safe. But what if we weren't. What if some snitch squealed on us? Oh, but nobody would do that, we were too popular. But what if we weren't as popular as we thought we were?

As I was busy giving myself a headache with all these conflicting thoughts, Lulu pinched my arm and hissed, "Make up your mind, Trixie. If we're gonna go, we've got to do it now. So are you in or not?"

Well, I was still pretty unsure about the whole thing, but Lulu was downright self-assured. She was so cool that it suddenly occurred to me she had done this a few ---- no, make that MANY ---- times before. Her confidence was contagious and spilling all over me. "Okay, Lulu Bell," my pet name for her, "let's do it!"

Of course, I wasn't the least bit hungry, having just wolfed down my half a Skippy peanut butter sandwich, bag of Fritos, Snickers candy bar, and three-cent carton of milk, but the thought of ditching a class was irresistible, even if it was only to the Gulp n Gobble. As soon as Miss Scaredy Sub turned away to confer with Millie, the piano player, Lulu and I hunkered down and scurried out the door. Once outside, and breathing a huge sigh of relief, Lulu and I stood up like normal people, squared our shoulders, and proceeded to calmly walk up the dirt path that led to Curley Street and the Gulp n Gobble.

As we made our way along the trail, I had visions of that scary, ugly French teacher, Mrs. Snotgrass, lurking behind the pine trees. Snotty, our nickname for her, was deviously waiting for me to get close enough, then she'd jump out, grab me by my delicate ear and drag my helpless body to the office of Mr. Rizzo, the assistant principal! The day wasn't all that warm, but I was sweating bullets! I removed my blue school sweater with the large gold "P" on the front, but even that didn't help. And what about Lulu, the innocent-looking pixie girl? She was as cool as a cucumber; not a drop of sweat on her.

We finally made it to the Gulp n Gobble, after about ten minutes, but I tell you, it was the longest ten minutes of my life! I was an absolute nervous wreck! Being terribly on edge, I knew I wouldn't be able to eat a thing, but Lulu announced she was going to get a triple-deck cheeseburger, large order of french fries, the largest cherry Coke they had, AND a hot fudge sundae for dessert! Talk about nerves of steel! And I never could figure out where she put it all - she was only five feet tall and weighed about ninety pounds soaking wet. Just the thought of all that grub on my swirling innards made me want to puke, but since Lulu was so hungry, I anxiously agreed to go in and sit with her while she gorged herself.

Approaching the double glass doors of the greasy spoon, we suddenly stopped dead in our tracks. Then we turned to each other in horror! There, sitting calmly at a corner table by himself, munching on a foot-long hot dog with extra onions, was our own chorus teacher! Luckily for us, Mr. Campbell was so engrossed in his chewing he had no idea we were frozen at the door, unable to move, lest we rouse him from his pigging out.

At last we came to our senses, turned on our heels and began racing lickety-split down the hill, back to the school. All thoughts of ice cream and Cokes flew out the window as we hightailed it back to our refuge. Huffing and puffing, we decided to hide behind some trash cans until the bell rang and the area would once again be crowded with kids.

Returning to normal breathing and enthusiastically congratulating each other on our great escape, we were startled out of our celebration by an unpleasant rasp. "Hey, you two! What are you doing crouched behind those trash cans like a couple of ninnies?"

Startled and bolting upright, I looked to see who owned that snarky voice. "Oh, hi, Cheery. Hi, Gil. Uh . . . not much. Lulu lost something and we were trying to find it," I said, thinking quickly on my feet, as usual.

"Really?" Then turning to Lulu, snoopy Cheery asked, "What did you lose, Lulu?"

Seeing Lulu begin to stammer, I immediately cut in. "None of your beeswax, Cheery! Now run along . . . oh, by the way, what are you and Gil doing out here? Don't you guys have a class now?"

That shut her up. "C'mon, Gil. Let's get away from these nuts!" Gil, always the obedient boyfriend, followed without a word. That got rid of them and they stalked off, but not toward the school. Toward the Gulp n Gobble.

When the bell rang to change classes, we came out of our hiding place and darted to our respective classes. For me it was geometry, complete with Pop McNultie standing outside his room. In a strange way, I found that reassuring. Some things hadn't changed, despite my short-lived descent into darkness. I wasn't proud of my delinquent actions, but I'm sure anyone can see how none of it was my fault. The blame lies squarely with two individuals ---- Lulu and Mr. Campbell. Lulu, because she tried to corrupt me, and Mr. Campbell, because . . . well, if he'd been in class like he was supposed to be, I never would have been tempted to ditch.

So, here's hoping my story will be a wake up call to any young Squirrel who might be headed down that same slippery slope of juvenile delinquency. You're welcome, Purdy High!

# BABYSITTING BLUNDER

The halls of good ol' Purdy High were crowded as usual as I finally made it to my long, green locker to fetch my half a Skippy peanut butter sandwich, bag of Fritos and Snickers candy bar. I was deep in concentration thinking about the geometry test I'd probably just flunked when, out of the blue, a big man appeared at my side and quietly said, "Trixie, I need to talk to you in private. Can you drop by my office today after school?" Then, without waiting for a reply, he hurried off down the hallway.

That big guy was Mr. Cole Goodman, aka Coach Goodman, one of the neatest teachers ever to roam the halls of PHS! I didn't have any idea what he wanted to talk to me about but remembering my recent history of goof-ups, my mind started going to the dark side.

The whole rest of the day I worried. Had Lulu Dilly let it slip about our one-hour vacation from Mr. Campbell's girls chorus class? Did Kitty Shrub rat me out about our archery contest?

Had Margery Sweetum bragged about our escapade in the boys locker room? Or was there even more damage to the drivers ed car? There were so many things I could be in trouble for ---- none of them my fault, of course!

The school day finally ended, about fifty hours longer than normal, so I slowly dragged myself to the office of Coach Goodman, deep in the bowels of the boys gym. To be perfectly honest I could have found my way there, with my eyes closed, simply by following my nose, if you get my drift. My knees were knocking so badly that even before my fist reached the door, Coach Goodman hollered, "Come in!"

To my great relief, Coach had a smile on his face. Well, it wasn't actually a smile, but rather that thing he did with his mouth that passed for a smile.

"Hi, Mr. Goodman, what's up?"

"Well, Trixie, Mrs. Goodman and I want to take in a movie Saturday night at the Moose Theater. We're going to see Lawrence of Arabia. It's our sixth anniversary, you see. I was wondering if you might want to babysit Corky, our son. He's five."

Oh, is that all?! A babysitting job. Here I was, afraid I was going to get kicked out of Purdy for some terrible transgression, or I was going to get thrown out of school on account of failing geometry, but Coach was simply asking me to babysit his tot!

"You bet I can!" I enthusiastically replied. "Not to brag, Mr. Goodman, but everyone considers me to be the best babysitter in Purdy. I'm always available on short notice, even on a Friday or Saturday night." That was true. I was certainly the most in demand. I wasn't really sure why, but I often overheard comments such as " . . . such a simple mind . . . can play Candy Land for hours . . . tells jokes only a five-year-old would laugh at . . . enjoys Mr. Potato Head more than the children ----" These nice compliments meant a lot to me, so I did my best to live up to the parents' great expectations.

The big anniversary night arrived and Coach picked me up at my house on Fairgrounds Avenue. Queenie, my German Shepherd, really liked him and started licking Coach's face. When we got back to his home, I finally got to meet Corky. The squirmy, redheaded, freckle-faced urchin was sprawled on the living room floor, covered in Tinker Toys.

"Hi-ya, Corky. My name's Trixie. What would you like to do tonight?" I asked, tousling the little guy's hair.

Hearing my icebreaker and knowing their son was in the most responsible hands possible, the oldsters gave Corky a goodby kiss and headed out the door.

Corky and I had barely started constructing Dracula out of Tinker Toys when there was a knock at the door. "You stay here, Corky, and let me see who it is." I cautiously opened the front door and, much to my delight, there stood my good buddies, Margery Sweetum and Sugar Wiggins. We were all in Mrs. Lafleur's drama class together. Even so, I knew I was not to let anyone in the house. Closing the door behind me, I went out on the front porch to talk to them.

Margie and Sugar were as surprised to see me as I was to see them. "Oh, hi, Trixie. What are you doing here? This isn't your house. Wanna buy a chocolate bar to support the drama club?" asked Margie. Sugar started pulling one out of a cardboard box.

"I'm here babysitting and why would I want to buy one of YOUR chocolate bars, Margie? I have a whole box of them to sell myself. The only way I'll be able to get rid of all mine is to buy them myself. So . . . to answer your question, no, I do not want to buy one of your stupid chocolate bars!"

"Well!" snorted Margie. "You don't have to have a cow! I didn't even know you were here babysitting. If I had, I never would have bothered to ----"

At that moment, we all heard it. A loud "click" that came from the other side of the door. Margie, Sugar and I silently stared at each other, as we listened to sounds of giggling coming from inside the house. It was pretty clear what had happened: that little rascal, Corky, had locked the door ---- and yours truly ---- out of the house!

Slightly panic-stricken, I immediately hollered at the door. "Corky Goodman, open this door right now!" More snickering from inside. At that point, Margie and Sugar decided to take their boxes of candy bars and leave me standing alone on the porch. I think Margie was still mad that I hadn't forked over my hard-earned dough to buy one of HER chocolate bars. As they scrambled down the front steps and took off down the road, they waved behind them, yelling, "Have fun babysitting!"

I tried the front door once more, but still no luck. Now I was becoming frantic, trying to think of how I'd get in. Then I remembered a kitchen window that had been left open, due to the earlier dinner of slightly nauseating (in my humble opinion) liver and onions. I quickly ran to the window, started to reach through the opening with both hands to pull myself in, when suddenly a little carrot top appeared and slammed the window shut, barely missing my fingers!

"Corky, that wasn't funny at all! You could have amputated all my digits!" I screamed at him through the glass.

"Sorry, Trixie. I didn't know it'd come down so fast. And not only could it have done what you said, but it could have cut your fingers off, too!" Then as he began wiggling around on the counter top, his right foot kicked a huge canister of flour, tipping it over and spilling flour all over the floor. I watched in wild-eyed horror as Corky began sliding, head first, onto the kitchen floor.

Not believing my eyes and fearing that my charge was injured, I put my face to the window and continued with my screeching! "Corky, are you okay? Speak to me! Say something so I know you're not hurt!"

In response to my shrieks of panic, I heard from the floor, "Trixie, you're so silly. Why do you think I'm hurt?" The little squirt was rolling around in the flour and splaying his arms and legs. "Look, Trixie! I'm making flour-angels!" He was having more fun than a barrel of monkeys.

"That's enough, Corky. Now let me in." But I was now talking to an empty room.

What to do? What to do? It was getting pretty dark out, but as I glanced around the yard, I spotted it! Propped against the backyard tool shed was an eighteen-foot ladder. I knew the house had a fireplace, so if I could only get on the roof . . . I carried the heavy ladder to the house, then carefully leaned it against the back porch. Ever so slowly I climbed the wooden rungs, until I made it to the roof. I warily crawled over to the chimney and peered down into it. Since my measurements were the same from top to bottom, I figured I'd be able to shoot down, with no protruding obstructions, in one fell swoop! Lowering my legs into the sooty tunnel, I raised my hands high above my head, then hollered "Geronimo!"

I'd never tried sliding down a chimney before, so this was indeed a new experience for me. I had no idea how much fun it could be! Even though I'd landed at the bottom ON my bottom, I thought about going back up and doing it again. However, always the professional, I reminded myself that my babysitting duties came first.

After wiping most of the soot from my eyes with the back off my hand, I opened my peepers and discovered an excited Corky standing before me. When he realized it was his babysitter and not Santa Claus, Corky began clapping his hands and hopping around, all the while squealing repeatedly, "Do it again, Trixie! Do it again!"

Naturally I was covered from head to toe in black soot and ash, but that little skallywag thought I'd put on the best show he'd ever seen and jumped on me for a big hug. Of course he was still covered in an inch of white flour, so together we made one gigantic, powdery gray mess.

Corky continued to beg, "Do the chimney trick again, Trixie," but I gave him the babysitter's standard answer for "no," which was "maybe next time." Then I promised him a homemade cherry Kool-Aid popsicle, if he'd let me clean him up. He agreed. Works every time!

For the next couple of hours, Corky and I swept and dusted and mopped and scoured ---- not only the house, but ourselves as well. After that we calmly played a nice, quiet game of Old Maid, while scarfing down graham crackers and milk.

I was just getting ready to put Corky to bed, when Coach and Mrs. Goodman got home. They gave him a hug and wanted to know how the evening went. "Did you two do anything fun?" asked Mrs. Goodman. Corky began to giggle when a small piece of ash fluttered down and landed on Coach's head, but as the parents looked around, they seemed happy with what they saw. In fact they gave me a quarter tip and asked if I'd be available the following Saturday. Corky began jumping up and down, "Please, Trixie! We can play down-the-chimney again." Coach looked at me for an explanation, but I just shrugged as if to say, "Kids!"

So that's the story of my first time babysitting Corky. I've imparted many words of wisdom, but this is perhaps one of the most valuable. For all you Purdy High School Squirrels trying to earn a buck by babysitting, don't ever forget: Always keep one foot in the door! You're welcome, Purdy High!

# THRILLS AT THE
# YIPPEE COUNTY FAIR

Since I lived smack dab on the corner of Fair and Fairgrounds in peaceful Purdy, I considered myself an expert on the fairgrounds and everything having to do with it. From horse races to rodeos to county fairs, I appointed myself the official official. This title, which I took very seriously, meant that during the Yippee County Fair of 1962, I had many responsibilities which I, Trixie Poor, and I alone could handle.

One of the first areas of concern had to do with traffic on my street. Besides standing in the middle of the road, waving my arms, and hollering at people to slow down, I plopped myself down in a lawn chair out in front of my house and counted the cars as they drove by. By doing that, I could give an accurate count to Purdy's Chief of Police, Kurt Langley, who was not only an esteemed colleague, but a personal friend to boot. And by knowing how many cars had entered the fairgrounds, I could tell Chief exactly how many officers he needed for crowd control.

The second area of concern dealt with traffic violations. One of the worst infractions involved people parking their cars in front of our gate! This crime prevented my folks from being able to move their '49 Chevy out to the street and drive to the Dandy Food Basket for more Skippy peanut butter with which to make my school lunches. Even with my cardboard sign, painted in bright red letters ---- DO NOT PARK IN FRONT OF TRIXIE'S GATE ---- certain delinquents still felt the need to break the law. When such a felony occurred, I would tuck one of my homemade tickets under their windshield wiper, then give a copy to Chief Langley. This was a frustrating endeavor, since most people simply cackled loudly, crumpled them in a ball and tossed them in the street. No one ever said law enforcement was going to be easy, but I never expected this added chore of running all over the neighborhood to pick up those dang tickets, lest I be an accomplice to littering. For anyone attempting to follow in my selfless footsteps, I might add that windy days were the pits.

There were many miscellaneous violations, but the following were particularly egregious: Ralphie Tittsworth's windshield had bird poop smeared all over it, thereby impairing visibility. Unfortunately I had to let this slide, because I wasn't sure where the car had been parked. If it had been under my corner pine tree, I might be implicated, if they could prove the culprit had been one of my birds.

Hubert Button's rearview mirror had greasy french fry fingerprints all over it, another visibility infraction, and proof he spent way too much time at the Gulp n Gobble on Curley Street.

Good ol' Gil Snedley parked right in the middle of the street. Despite my better judgment I had to let this one go, because Gil had given me so many rides, and his girlfriend, Cheery Perkins, was my good chum. I only hoped I wouldn't be found guilty of corruption later on, but since we hadn't conspired for him to park all goofy like that, I figured the charge wouldn't stick.

Finally, after half a day of policing my street, I was approached by Chief Langley, who thanked me for my efforts, but INSISTED I run along and join the throng of fairgoers inside the fairgrounds. I presented him with my detailed list of violations and assured him that Fairgrounds Avenue was safe from crime, barring the occasional Juicy Fruit or Bazooka gum wrapper recklessly flung into the street. He thanked me profusely, then again INSISTED I go to the fair with my friends. Sufficiently confident that the area around my house was under control, I gave Chief Langley a hug, then skipped over to the fairgrounds entrance gate.

As much as I loved the fair, there were some activities, the ones involving ribbons, that I didn't care for at all. Had I ever won so much as an honorable mention with any of my entries, I might have felt differently, but since the judges never saw fit to award me even a measly atta-girl,

I steadfastly assured myself that the exhibition halls were worthless. For example, I didn't have any animals to show, except for my German Shepherd, Queenie. Year after year, Queenie was disqualified in the cows and pigs competitions. I found this to be quite unfair. What difference was there, really, between a cow, a pig, and a dog? The only thing that came to my mind was that a cow or pig wouldn't be welcome on your bed, as Queenie was on mine. And then there was the crabapple pie incident. One year I entered a delicious-looking, I thought, crabapple pie, but all the dumbbell judges took one look at it and rudely refused to taste it. All except one, who, shortly after sampling my rare pastry, was stricken with severe stomach cramps and hauled off to the Yippee County Hospital. There was speculation that my pie was to blame, but to this day I affirm it was that tenth cotton candy he inhaled that pushed him over the edge. And finally, there was the lovely apron I'd so diligently sewn out of burlap. It had been mistaken for a HAT by those bird-brain, half-blind judges. Good grief! How did my entries stand a chance, when they were being judged by such incompetents? Obviously, they didn't! Therefore I shunned the exhibition buildings and instead made a beeline for the midway, where all the worthwhile action was.

As I was strolling along toward the Ferris wheel, I ran into my two best friends, Margie and Bonita. "C'mon, Trixie!" they exclaimed. "We're gonna ride some rides!

Wanna join us? Just try not to throw up all over everything like the last time you rode the merry-go-round!"

Humph! That remark was uncalled for; true, but uncalled for. I haughtily informed them that I no longer got sick on the rides and that, just to prove it, we should all go on the Ferris wheel together. They held back for a sec, frowned in indecision, then double-dog-dared each other to ride with me. With that we all scrunched together in a chair.

Well, I was doing great! Not even a hint of puking, much to the girls' relief. We made one full rotation and were halfway through the second, when all of a sudden the wheel let out a screeching sound and came to an alarmingly abrupt halt! All the riders began screaming in a panic! The carnie, way down below, was doing his best to get the wheel started again, but nothing was happening. Then I heard cries from everywhere: "Trixie, help us! We're stuck! You're the only one who can save us! Get us down!"

"Hang on, everybody! I know what to do!" I shouted, displaying enormous courage, with no regard whatsoever for my own personal safety.

I sprang into action! I threw the safety bar up and made a spectacular leap to the cross brace member. After a half spin, I reached out and grabbed the main support beam with my left hand and pivoted over to the lateral spoke. The spoke was quite greasy and caused me to slide down about five feet, until I got a foothold on the girder truss. From there I swung hand over hand, silently thanking Muller

Valley Elementary for the monkey bars, while grabbing every turn buckle and cable rigging as they came along! Down I went, as stranded thrill-seekers cheered me on, not to mention every single person who was at the fair! At long last I neared the bottom, legs swinging every which way, until I accidentally kicked the carnie in the head and knocked him out cold!

Amid ear-shattering shouts of encouragement, I stood on the control platform, determined to restart the emergency catline. I engaged the spindle pulley and depressed the hydraulic clutch and ta-dah! The Ferris wheel began to turn!

Now I was in complete control, since the carnie had no idea where he was, or WHO he was, so I decided to give the riders their money's worth! I removed the speed stop and pushed the lever to full throttle! They were going to get the ride of their life, by golly! Faster and faster! Wheel racing round and round! Girls screaming with, what seemed to me, ecstatic delight! Boys bug-eyed with uncontrolled excitement! Everyone shouting, " More, More!" To tell the truth, I'm not exactly sure what they were yelling, since the contraption was roaring at 300 decibels, but they were flailing their arms at me as they flashed by, so I waved back, overjoyed to give them such a good time. I wished it could go on and on, but when smoke began billowing from the throwout bearing, I decided the kids had had enough thrills for a while. I reached for the throttle and noticed the red warning light flashing like a lunatic's eyes, and the handle so hot I could barely pull it back ---- but I did, of course, and sadly brought the unforgettable adventure to a halt.

As I offloaded the riders, I noticed that all the girls' hair was wind-blown straight back and that most of the kids who wore glasses no longer had them. And how had the cowboys' hats gotten scattered all over the midway? And why couldn't any of them walk in a straight line? And why were some of them kissing the ground or mumbling prayers of thanks? I tell you, there are so many mysteries in this world.

So there you have it. That's the story of how I saved the stranded riders and made it possible for a whole bunch of PHS kids to have a once-in-a-lifetime Ferris wheel ride at the Yippee County Fair! No need to thank me. You're welcome, Purdy High!

# ROCKIN' N ROLLIN'
# AT THE RADIO STATION

It was a nippy fall evening as I was slaving away in La Belle Beauty Shop straightening up after the best beautician in Purdy, Sissy Applebaum. Sissy had hired me on the spot after her regular cleaning lady, Mrs Emmaline Spruce, had up and quit, after Mrs. Spruce's husband was found guilty of bootlegging and sent off to the pokey. Rumor had it that Mrs. Spruce was going to take over the family business. I was exuberant at the thought of landing a job that paid more than my fifty-cent-an-hour babysitting jobs. This one paid a whole dollar! Not only did this gig pay more, but I was told by Sissy that there was room for advancement if my cleaning skills proved to be exceptional, which I was confident they would. This new career was more than enough to sustain me in Saturday afternoon movies, accompanied by salted, buttered popcorn.

As I was disinfecting the combs in a smelly, pink solution, I considered doing the same thing to the brushes, but then I thought to myself, why bother? They looked fine to me ---- a few greasy hairs here and there, but nothing catastrophic. Besides, I rarely washed my brush at home and had never had a lice problem. Well . . . there was that one time, but it had nothing to do with my brush, I'm sure. My mom was very upset because she was worried my German Shepherd, Queenie, would get those blood-suckers, too, but fortunately Queenie must have been immune, because all she ever attracted was the wayward flea.

I was also contemplating the world's situation while I performed my chores. By "world's situation," I meant pondering the likelihood of Purdy High winning the home football game Saturday night against our biggest rival, the Podunk Skunks from Podunk High. Podunk was situated about one hundred miles north of Purdy and claimed to be about the same size, both in population and area. I assert that Purdy was bigger and better in everything. For eons the two schools had collided in fierce competitions. But regarding the game, deep down inside, I knew we probably wouldn't win since we Purdy Squirrels lost every game we ever played, with the exception of that dramatic homecoming game a few weeks earlier, where we'd slaughtered Furnace City's Central High 20-18!

To take my mind off Saturday night's upcoming game and to make my job more enjoyable, not that scrubbing the toilet wasn't a heck of a lot of fun in its own right, I always played my newfangled, Japanese, transistor radio.

I'd received this mind-boggling innovation for Christmas the year before and it had turned out to be, without a doubt, one of the greatest presents I'd ever gotten in my whole entire life! But, the way it functioned was a complete mystery to me. I could sort of understand how a radio might work if it were plugged in but how it could work, just sitting all by itself, on top of a counter, was beyond me. Every day, before I left home to walk to the shop, I'd take out the battery and touch it to my tongue to make sure it hadn't died. I always got a small shock, but that was a minor price to pay for being assured that my radio was up and running. I didn't even want to think about not having it at my place of employment; that would have been devastating!

My favorite radio station, in fact the only station I could get on my transistor, was Purdy's own KNUT 97.3, which, as luck would have it, was located right next door to the beauty shop on Muller Valley Road. Whenever I had the shop's door open to air out the suffocating permanent wave and dye smells, I could listen to KNUT without even using my radio. Sometimes, when I was outside frantically shaking out the dust mop full of dead hair and other such crud, I'd catch a glimpse of the DJ sitting in front of a stack of records. I'd flap my mop in his direction and we'd cordially wave to each other. I'm absolutely positive he thought I was the owner of the shop, since I always acted so mature for my age.

One pleasant evening, I was humming along with Elvis

as he belted out Hound Dog while I scoured the sink as hard as was humanly possible to the beat of the song. In the blink of an eye, the DJ from next door suddenly burst into my shop, arms flailing like a drowning lunatic. As I stood transfixed, unable to move, he began approaching me. With foamy spit oozing down his chin, he managed to sputter, "Hey, kid, I need your help! There's been . . . uh . . . some kind of . . . uh . . . emergency at my house and I . . . uh . . . have to rush home! I want you to . . .uh . . . run the station . . .uh . . . while I go home for a couple of hours! Do you . . . uh . . . think you can do that?!"

"Do you think you can do that?" What a nutty question to ask me! Naturally I could do that! What couldn't I do, other than the occasional cursed geometry problem? Waggling my fingers at the distraught lad, I told him, "You just run along and do what you have to do. I can certainly manage a hick station like dinky KNUT." Well, I didn't use those exact words, since he was a lot bigger than little ol' me. He hesitated for a moment, mumbled something that sounded like "beggars can't be choosers," then ran lickety-split out the door to his yellow VW bug.

Hot diggity dog! I'd always wanted to be a DJ and now I had my very own show! It was my big break! I wondered if this was how the famous Mr. Dick Clark had gotten his start. Every Saturday afternoon, I'd adjust the rabbit ears on our black and white television set, grab a bag of Fritos, then settle back to watch American Bandstand. Sometimes I'd even dance along with Joey or Maria as

Dick played songs or had a real live band for those cool kids in Philadelphia, or Philly, as we regulars liked to call it. Frankly, I was never quite sure where Philadelphia was, but I knew it was definitely somewhere east of Podunk or south of Furnace City.

Realizing there must be dead air at the station, I hurriedly tossed my scrub brush on the floor and flipped the "closed" sign on Sissy's front door. I had bigger fish to fry! My sights were set on becoming Purdy's newest, and BEST, disc jockey! Philadelphia, here I come!

As I positioned myself behind the mounds of 45s and adjusted the microphone, the station's telephone immediately began ringing off the hook with song requests. The first request came from Clarence Waddle, Bonita's on-again off-again boyfriend. He wanted me to play Moon River, Bonita's favorite tune, because he was again in the dog house with Bonita and was trying to get on her good side. Well, I looked and I looked, but that doggone record was nowhere to be found, so I did the only sensible thing I could think of. I began singing! Every Purdy High Squirrel knew the words to Moon River since it was played at least a million times a day, so I simply took advantage of my natural-born talent and began crooning as loud as I could into the microphone: "Moooon Riiiver -----"

Suddenly stricken with an acute case of rudeness, Clarence started hollering, "Knock it off, Trixie! You're making my ears bleed!"

"Humph!" I snorted, then promptly hung up on Mr.

Oaf. Bonita was most assuredly going to get some serious advice in the romance department the next time I talked to her!

Moving right along, I took the next caller, who happened to be the quirky Ralphie Tittsworth. Ralphie wanted to hear his favorite tune, "The Battle of New Orleans." Once again I couldn't find the record. Well, who could?! They all looked alike! Since I couldn't remember the words very well, I asked Ralphie if he'd care to do the honors. Convinced he sounded exactly like Johnny Horton, Ralphie proudly and loudly began bellowing in some unknown key: "In 1918 we took a little trip, along with Colonel Sanders down the mighty Sippissip, we took a box of chicken and we ate some collard greens, and we met the bloody British in the town of New Orleans ----- well . . . we . . ."

"Stop it!" I squawked. "If you don't know the words and you can't sound like a human person, instead of an injured bovine, then get off the phone! Go pig out on some barnyard fowl and grass clippings and call me back when you're not half-starved!" To that I heard, "Big dumb nut!" followed by the dial tone. Another "humph" by me.

Since the musical part of my show wasn't going too hot, I decided to switch to the news. The only news I was aware of was what had gone on at Purdy High that day, so I figured I go with that.

"Good evening, all you KNUT listeners! Welcome to The Trixie Show, coming to you from the beautiful

Half-Mile-High Town of Purdy! Here are the news highlights of the day: Pop McNultie was out sick, so we had a substitute. Great news for students, especially me, because the geometry test was postponed indefinitely. Meatloaf and mashed potatoes were served in the cafeteria, unless you brought your own sack lunch of half a Skippy peanut butter sandwich, a bag of Fritos, and a Snickers candy bar, like I did. Winnie Ragsdale and Sugar Wiggins got into trouble in Mr. Reinagle's typing class for chewing a whole pack of Juicy Fruit all at once. The kindly Mr. Reinagle later admitted to somewhat overreacting, due to his great concern about a wad falling out of their mouths and clogging up the keys. He stated that perhaps his fear had been irrational. I didn't think so. I'd seen the way those girls chomped on that gum! Continuing on a personal note, yours truly again got sent to Mr. Rizzo's office for talking in Mrs. Snotgrass's French class. I was speaking in English, so that's probably why. And one of my best friends got mad at her boyfriend because he was leaning "provocatively" ---- my word of the day ---- against another girl's locker. Sorry I can't tell you their last names, but journalists don't have to reveal stuff they don't want to. You could have Police Chief Langley toss me in the Yippee County Jail, but even then I wouldn't tell you! My integrity, as a reporter, is way too important! So there you have the important news of the day. Now back to the tunes! All the tunes, all the time -----"

I was just reaching for the phone, in order to

vocalize another request, when into my studio charged the aforementioned DJ, only this time he appeared to be even more hysterical than previously. It seems he'd been listening to The Trixie Show on his car radio, while speeding home to the emergency, when he concluded that the "emergency situation" at the radio station was a lot more critical than the one he was racing to (whatever that was supposed to mean) so he turned his Bug around in the middle of Curley Hill and came barreling back.

I calmly informed him I was available anytime to do my show. Except after my 9:30 bedtime; or during school hours; or on Wednesday nights, because of church choir practice; or when I had Rainbow meetings on certain Tuesdays; or when I was doing volunteer work at the Yippee County Hospital; or when I was babysitting the town's rugrats. And, of course, when I was maintaining the beauty shop. I also let him know that if he wanted to work with me, we'd have to call it The Trixie and That Other DJ Show.

DJ took all my demands in stride, surprisingly enough, and told me he'd let me know. As he purposefully gripped my arm and escorted me back to La Belle Beauty Shop, I couldn't help but reflect upon his remarkable self-control. After all, a few more minutes with me doing my show and that poor guy could easily have been replaced! Good thing his boss hadn't been listening and heard how great I was!

So, that's the story of how I came this close ---- picture

thumb and index finger nearly touching ---- to becoming the best DJ west of Philadelphia and how I kept the Squirrel's favorite radio station on the air! You're welcome, Purdy High!

# DRAMA AT THE MOOSE THEATER

It was a warm Saturday afternoon in good ol' Purdy when Margie Sweetum, Sugar Wiggins and I were honing our outstanding acting skills at my house on Fairgrounds Avenue. We were working on a scene from Lassie Come Home that our drama teacher, Mrs. Edith Lafleur, had chosen for us. Being the best actresses in the school, especially me, we knew that with a little luck we'd make it big in Hollywood. Naturally, I was playing the lead, Timmy. Margie and Sugar were playing Timmy's parents. My dog, Queenie, was Lassie. It was a bit of a stretch for Queenie, since she was a German Shepherd, but she barked right on cue and raised her paw when directed to do so. All things considered, she gave an award-winning performance. Though Queenie didn't look like Lassie (Queenie was prettier!), Margie resembled Vivian Leigh, while Sugar favored Raquel Welch. I, of course, looked exactly like Debbie Reynolds, my idol from the stupendous

"Tammy" movie productions. Sugar thought I looked like Timmy.

Having perfected our scenes, I suggested to the girls that we go downtown to the Moose Movie Theater. "Did you guys know Brides of Dracula is now showing? It's going to win the Oscar for Best Picture! I just know it . . . unless Tammy does. Maybe Mrs. Lafleur will give us extra credit, because watching Dracula suck all the blood out of the beautiful maiden would be a great way to enhance our drama studies!" For once they agreed with me so, hollering goodby to my mom, off we went.

The best way to get from my house to downtown, if you didn't drive or didn't feel like walking, was to take the Purdy Stage. This was a small bus that made a loop all around the town and would stop right on the corner by my house. Buckshot was the driver's name and he was a real nice guy, except he had one tiny flaw: He was always picking his nose. Every time I was outside and the little white bus would drive by, I'd wave to Buckshot. Removing his index finger from a nostril, he'd cordially wave back. My mother said he was "digging for gold," which I thought sounded much nicer than "picking a booger." I'm not exactly sure why, but I never liked that word, booger, and tried never to use it. Anyway, as Margie, Sugar and I were waiting for the bus, I warned them about that finger. "Whatever you do, don't come in contact with Buckshot's fingers," I cautioned. Then I clarified, "In particular, the second finger. Simply place your dime in the palm of his hand or hold the dime by the very edge to give it to him."

"You're one of the nuttiest kids I've ever known in my whole life, Trixie! I've known you since first grade and, I swear, you get nuttier every year, if that's at all possible," remarked Sugar, in what I considered to be a very snide manner. Evidently, Margie had nothing to add to that nonsensical statement. She merely stood there rolling her eyes at me. Well, I was quite used to that, and she was far from the first to do it, so what did I care?

"Fine! If you two gooney birds want to live dangerously and contract some kind of devastating illness from touching those gross finger germs, then it's okay by me. Just don't come blubbering to me when you're in the hospital, covered with hideous turquoise scabs, and unable to pronounce your own name!" I directed my comments to both of them, since I had the feeling they were ganging up on me.

"Settle down, Trixie. Okay, we'll try not to touch his trigger finger. Now, are you happy?"

Actually, yes, I was. I felt confident that I'd extended their lives by several years.

We all made it onto the bus without incident and, in about fifteen minutes, the Purdy Stage dropped us off in front of the Moose Theater. Crossing our fingers that we hadn't missed the beginning, we each paid a quarter to get in. I then splurged on a nickel box of popcorn; Margie bought a Big Hunk; and Sugar got herself a Chunky and a pack of Blackjack chewing gum. I loved that gum, too, but I couldn't afford it along with the popcorn. Sugar very generously said I could have a piece of hers. Those girls could be pretty nice when they wanted to be and when they weren't arguing with me over the dangers, or lack thereof, of snotty fingers.

As we made our way into the sumptuous theater, full of plush, velvet, burgundy-colored seats, we were relieved to see that the lights were still on. That meant we hadn't missed the adorable Woody Woodpecker, my favorite cartoon, or the all-important previews of coming attractions. The boring black and white newsreels I could do without. I got enough of that in Mr. Peabody's history class.

Sugar and Margie immediately sat down and began scarfing down their snacks. Frankly, it was embarrassing the way they acted like they hadn't eaten in a year. I gave my popcorn to Sugar for safe-keeping, telling her she could only have a stick-of-gum's-worth. Then I started looking around to see who was there.

Several rows back I spotted Bonita and Clarence, holding hands. This came as a huge shock to me since last I heard, they'd broken up. I wondered how they'd gotten back together again. "Hey, Bonita," I hollered. "I see you've forgiven Clarence for flirting with Kitty Shrub in typing class. Did he come groveling to you on all fours? I hope so! It was so bad Mr. Reinagle even had to tell him to keep his hands off Kitty's keyboard!"

Bonita gave Clarence a bewildered, then scathing, look and quickly snatched her hand back. Then she turned to face Mayor Floyd Toot on the other side, keeping her back to Clarence. I was a little surprised to see His Honor at a Dracula movie, however this only confirmed my point about Dracula winning an Oscar. It appealed to everyone, young and . . . extremely . . . old.

As I continued to survey the audience, way in the back I could barely see Ralphie Tittsworth with, of all people, Winnie Ragsdale. I didn't even know they were dating. Was I the last to know about everything? Needing to know more, I cupped my hands, then yelled as loud as I could, "HELLO, Ralphie and Winnie! I didn't know you guys were seeing each other! How long has this been going on? And why wasn't I informed?"

They barely nodded at me, then scrunched way down in their seats so I could no longer see them. Obviously, etiquette was no longer taught in the schools and, unfortunately, we were seeing the results of such an oversight right now. If this was a sign of the times, I lamented, then manners would soon be a thing of the past. It seemed like some of these kids were being raised by wolves!

As I was pondering the demise of civilization, who did I happen to see way up in the balcony? Why, Cheery Perkins and Gil Snedly, of course! When they weren't at the Neckin Drive-In, it was common knowledge around Purdy that this is where you could find them on weekend afternoons. Realizing they probably hadn't seen me yet, I began frantically waving my arms to get their attention. Gil slowly began sinking into his plush, velvet, burgundy-colored seat. "Hey Gil and Cheery!" I shouted, while continuously flailing my arms. "Are we going to the drive-in tonight?" No response. After the third time of screaming their names at the top of my lungs, I finally got a feeble wave from Cheery, at the same moment Gil shot upright as though he'd been poked in the ribs with a stick. Since they seemed to be having such a hard time hearing me, I was going to suggest they visit the school nurse first thing Monday morning. Perhaps Mrs. Shott could give them a miracle pill to clear up their hearing loss. I certainly hoped so; they were so young. With any luck, it would be nothing more than gooey wax build-up.

Turning my attention away from the balcony, where it was apparently too hard for anyone to hear me, I started scanning the main floor again. Everywhere I looked I was seeing kids I knew, but they didn't seem to see me. It was rather frustrating, so I did what any normal person in a movie theater would do: I waved my arms back and forth with all my might and yelled their names until I practically gave myself a severe case of laryngitis! As the lights began to dim, Margie and Sugar each grabbed one of my arms and ordered me to sit down. "Stop making a spectacle of yourself, Trixie, and embarrassing US along the way!" Margie exclaimed. "Sugar and I wanted to move someplace else, but every seat's taken. And, of course, no one would trade with us without a substantial amount of money trading hands, which we didn't have. Now SIT DOWN once and for all!"

I harrumphed once or twice, then sat down. Big deal. I was going to sit down anyway ---- Woody Woodpecker was on the screen! And after that, Dracula! Plus I needed to pig out on my popcorn, before it got cold.

We'd laughed and laughed at Woody, but from the moment the actors' names appeared on the screen in that blood-red color, I was scared out of my wits! Peter Cushing was born to play Dracula and I couldn't possibly imagine anyone getting the Best Actor Oscar but him! Paul Newman, Robert Redford and Clint Eastwood were kind of cute, in their own way, and popular with most of the girls, but I can tell you right now that not one of them could hold a candle to Peter Cushing. If he didn't win the Academy Award, I had every intention of starting a protest, possibly even picketing the Moose Theater! I'd never considered myself a revolutionist, but some causes demand that I take a stand. Besides, I had this strong, psychic feeling that those other three would probably be has-beens by the time they turned thirty.

Everything was progressing nicely in the film. Count Dracula had turned a couple of clueless gals into vampires, but the lovely baroness continued to evade him and his pointy teeth. Then just as we were getting to the really spooky part ---- the part where Dracula bites the baroness's jugular vein, because the ninny was too much of a lame-brain to wear a garlic necklace around her stupid neck ---- we heard that ominous, all-too-familiar sound coming from the projection booth: clackety, clackety, clackety, clac . . . Yep! The film had broken!

As anyone knows, who's ever sat in a theater and had the film break at a crucial moment, things can get ugly real fast! First the hushed complaints; then the murmured boos; then the louder boos, coupled with hisses; and then the inevitable violence ---- empty paper cups, popcorn kernels, and Milk Duds thrown at the screen! I knew things would only go downhill from there so, in a flash, I sprang into action! I bolted from my seat, ran to the stage and, following in the steps of that portly director, Mr. Alfred Hitchcock, began clapping my hands. "Attention! Mrs. Lafleur's drama students! On stage! Now!" I commanded, with all the authority I could muster.

Immediately Margie and Sugar jumped up and raced to join me on stage, followed by Bonita, Winnie, Ralphie and Hubert. I don't know where Hubert came from. I'd looked for him earlier, to no avail, after somebody said they'd seen him. Oh well, he was here now. I began shouting directions! "Sugar, you're the baroness! Bonita, you're the butler who distracts Dracula . . . and speaking of distracting . . . pay attention . . . quit looking around for Clarence! Ralphie you're the understudy for all the parts; Margie, you're the maid who drives the stake through Dracula's heart! The rest of you actors are the terrified villagers." I gave them a minute to absorb my assignments, then loftily added,

"I, of course, shall be executing the role of the menacing Count Dracula!"

"Why do you always get to have the big parts, Trixie? And I don't want to be the maid," whined Margie. "I want to get my neck bitten by Dracula. My part's too small and I think ----"

"Margie Sweetum," I scolded. "Mrs. Lafleur says there's no such thing as a crummy part, just a crummy actor, or actress ---- as the case may be." I paused to stare at her with squinty, emerald green eyes for a full fifteen seconds, in order to get my point across. "So grab that cotton candy cone off the floor and get ready to stab Dracula in the heart with it!"

Turning my attention to the rest of the cast, I continued, "Now the rest of you people, listen up! We've got one chance, and one chance only, to do this scene, so make it good and make Mrs. Lafleur and me proud!" Then I took off my penny loafers, slapped the heels together, yelled 'Action!' and directed the unfolding drama: Dracula (me) stalks the baroness across the stage, baring my wicked fangs; Sugar . . . er, I mean . . . the baroness is frozen in fear, as I raise my arms, ready to pounce; Margie . . . er, the maid . . . enters stage left, screams to draw my attention away from Sugar, gives Bonita . . . uh, the butler . . . the chance to push me to the floor. That last bit of action, by the way, was a lot harder than necessary. Margie said Bonita was miffed because I'd told her about Clarence in the typing class. Anyway, the maid . . . um, I mean

Margie . . . um, no, I mean the maid . . . pounds the cotton candy cone with her fist and voila! I'm dead for good! Rats! I mean, Dracula's dead for good!

Well, the audience went wild! We received a standing ovation for, I'm pretty sure, at least thirty minutes. Everybody, including the Honorable Mayor Toot, was shouting, "Encore! Encore!" Most of the fans had tears of joy streaming down their cheeks. When the cheers started to die down, the wobbly-kneed manager, Toby something-or-other, stepped onto the stage and made the following announcement: "Ladies and gentlemen, as manager of the Moose Theater, I am eternally grateful to Trixie and the drama students for preventing what could have been one of the worst riots in the history of Purdy. As such, I am issuing a free pass to each member of the cast for next Saturday's matinee."

All the kids began jumping up and down and hugging each other. I thought that was a nice gesture on Toby's part, but I knew the matinee was going to be Horror of Dracula, which I'd already seen a couple of years before at the Neckin Drive-In. Then I thought, I'll go anyway. It might be interesting to see it sitting down, not standing in the drizzle with my left ear to the speaker. The kids I'd gone with had said I talked too much and had kicked me out of the car. Besides, I'd forgotten how the movie ended.

Then Toby carried on with his words of praise, looking directly at me, "And for Trixie, the best director since Mr.

Hitchcock, I'm throwing in a free box of popcorn!" I took an appropriate bow, smiling ever-so modestly.

With Toby's thank-you speech over with, the thespians congratulated each other on a job well done. I'm not trying to slight the others, but it's clear as a bell that I was the one who saved the Moose Theater from total destruction and I was the one who organized a play in which the Purdy drama students could shine. I'm simply clarifying the facts. You're welcome, Purdy High!

# SURVIVING
# THE SCIENCE CLASSES

On the whole, my four-year sentence served at good ol' Purdy High in the early Sixties went pretty well. The only time I wanted to be pardoned was when I had to take a science class. They were so boring, not like P.E. and chorus; and so pointless, not like geometry and Latin. But the powers that be were shoving them down our throats anyway, as if science were somehow going to help us in our daily lives. What a laugh!

In Mr. Bunson's biology class, I learned how a plant makes sugar from the sun. Who cares, except maybe the plant? And in chemistry, I had to memorize a bunch of jumbled up letters and numbers like $H_2O$ and $CO_2$. What a waste of noggin power. I wisely believed that my brain, having a limited space in which to learn things, should not be cluttered up with such nonsense, but be saved for much more important stuff, such as remembering what everyone wore at the Thanksgiving Turkey Trot dance or thinking up new tricks to teach Queenie. One day I got up the nerve to inform Mr. Bunson about the worthlessness of all those science classes. He produced a blank look for a very long time, shook his head slowly from side to side, then muttered, "Trixie, you have the IQ of a Neanderthal."

A Neanderthal! What a darn nice thing to say, considering my last comment. I always knew I liked Mr. Bunson, despite his chosen profession, and now I knew why! He was not above flattering someone, even when he was in the wrong. Just goes to show you ---- not all science teachers are fuddy-duddies.

There was another thing I didn't like about science and it was a biggie. It seemed that ninety-nine percent of the scientists were MEN! Being a forward-thinking, liberated woman akin to Lucy Ricardo, this fact didn't sit well with me. Oh sure, there was Marie Curie, but look what happened to that poor thing! And we never studied about any of their pitiful, long-suffering wives. I'll bet nobody even knows what Thomas Edison's wife's name was ----- and don't say MRS. Edison, smarty pants! Don't you just know SHE was the one baking him chocolate chip cookies, and ironing his underpants, and scrubbing all those test tubes so he could do all that "important inventing" which made him so famous and splashed him all over the history books! Oh, don't get me started! I could go on and on about the injustice, but I'd better get back to the topic at hand ---- cutting up dead animals.

At long last a science class came along I could really

sink my teeth into! We were going to dissect either a tiny pig or a cat. For non-scientific people, unlike yours truly, "dissect" is a fancy word for "cut up into little pieces." According to the teacher, the purpose of this surgery was to gain a knowledge of anatomy. I just thought it would be neat to see a cat from the inside out. Mr. Bunson was once again my teacher and he was thrilled about it. I know this because when he saw me sitting in his class again, he stared straight at me and said, "Oh, great. Trixie's back. Isn't this a fine kettle of fish?" Well, who doesn't love fish?

Naturally I was thrilled to be stuck in Mr. Bunson's class again - for two reasons: (1) because, as everyone could see, I was the teacher's pet and (B) because his son, Billy Bunson, was a good buddy of mine. I figured I'd be guaranteed an A+ if Billy was my partner. Unfortunately for me and my grade, Billy was a year older and not in my class, so I was headed for trouble.

Racking my brain for a solution to my indelicate problem ---- how to get a good grade without doing much, if any, work ---- I came up with a brilliant idea. I'd get Stanley Weiss, aka The Egg Head, to be my partner. Approaching Stanley outside the classroom, I offered him my proposal: "Hey, Stanley, how about you and me being partners on this cat thing?"

Stanley, way too dramatically it seemed to me, threw his hands way up in the air and screeched, "YOUR partner? What? Are you crazy? I want to get into college! Find yourself another patsy!" And with those nonsensical words resonating in my head, I watched him turn so quickly to enter the biology class, he nearly ran into the wall.

Humph! Think, Trixie, think . . . aha! Hubert Button. Not the brightest bulb in the chandelier, but always ready to do MORE than his fair share. Also, since his addiction to brownies was known far and wide, I hatched a scheme.

"Hi, Hubie," I whispered in my most seductive voice, learned from watching Gidget on our black and white TV. I was ready to pounce with my offering of brownies.

"Hi, kid. What's wrong with your voice? Laryngitis?"

"No, I don't have laryngitis, you goofball!" So much for seduction. "Do you have a cat partner or not, and if you don't, do you want to be mine? I'll bake you a batch of brownies."

Shrugging nonchalantly, Hubert replied, "Sure, why not. I like to live dangerously ---- and I like brownies."

So, Hubert Button and I became lab partners and were presented with our cat about the same time the notorious Purdy Cat Scandal story was broken. It seems some bigshots from the state's wildlife department were doing research around our little town and discovered "the skunk, possum, and raccoon populations had significantly and inexplicably declined" in the last few years. Since I'd also overheard Mr. Bunson complaining about the lack of funding for science projects, I wasn't exactly sure who we were whittling on, Bootsie or Pepe Le Pew.

As anyone could attest to who'd been in the science building during cut-up time, the smell was even worse than the boys locker room. How I know that shall remain a secret. Even if you weren't taking a science class, you could smell the stench of the formaldehyde all over campus. Thinking it had permeated their clothes, the girls were spritzing themselves with cheap colognes; the boys were trying to act cool, but crying when no one was looking; the teachers were crabbier than usual. All in all, it was a nightmare of colossal proportions.

Then one day, as Hubert and I were hacking away on poor Bootsie, or Pepe, as the case might have been, I happened to glance down at the floor of the classroom. There, by one of my penny loafers, which actually had a valuable mercury head dime in it instead of a penny, was a trickle of formaldehyde! Following the trail of the leak, I soon discovered its source ---- a hole in one of the cat vats. No wonder the place stunk to high heaven! I immediately stuck my thumb in the hole to prevent any further leakage, while shouting, "Mr. Bunson, come quick! I'm no Hans Brinker and the liquid pressure is starting to build! I'll stay here as long as necessary, of course, but my stamina can only last so long!"

Suddenly aware of my plight, Mr. Bunson came rushing over! "Oh, Trixie, you poor, dear, courageous thing! How did you find that hole? Here, let me help you!"

With those reassuring words echoing in my ears, I gratefully watched as Mr. Bunson quickly yanked off Ralphie Tittsworth's white sock. Ralphie had removed his brand new Buster Browns earlier, fearing the liquid would wreck them. Clutching the sock, Mr. Bunson then stuffed it into the ominous hole, thereby coining the phrase, "Put a sock in it."

Later that day, as I recounted my story to the editor of The Squirrelly Times, I repeated my assertion that my thumb had been poked in the vat hole for several hours. Hubert Button and the rest of the class, including Mr. Bunson, all claimed it had only been a couple of seconds. I will admit that I was a tad shaken up after that ordeal, so perhaps I was a few minutes off. I mean, who wouldn't be traumatized? There I stood on that cold, stinky floor, attempting to save my class, as well as the whole school, from the noxious fumes of that poison! We could all have perished! On the plus side, I concluded to the reporter, my thumb is so well preserved, it looks like it belongs to a five-year-old!

So that's the story of how I prevented everyone at PHS from being poisoned by formaldehyde. You're welcome, Purdy High!

# SABOTAGE AT THE PURDY LANES

I always thought bowling was the greatest thing since my Hollywood crush, Fabian, so when Miss Corey told my P.E. class that we were going to spend the next four weeks at the Purdy Bowling Lanes, I was in hog heaven! What an easy A+ for me! Kitty Shrub may have been proclaimed the best archer at PHS, thanks to my inability to recruit a reliable human target ---- one that wouldn't start blubbering hysterically the minute she saw me raise my bow and arrow ----- but I knew I could beat Kitty, and everybody else, at the challenging game of bowling! That may sound just a teensy bit cocky, but since my parents always told me to tell the truth, well . . .

My P.E. class had been practicing at Dottie Darlin's dad's (try saying that real fast three times) bowling establishment for a couple of weeks. Leaving from the high school, we girls would walk to the Purdy Bowling Lanes as a group, passing by the most popular greasy spoon in town, the Gulp n Gobble. Lulu Dilly's eyes would glaze over whenever she spotted the enticing colored posters of grub, especially the ones of hot fudge sundaes. I'd be forced to grab her skinny little arm and scold her, in my meanest motherly voice: "Don't even THINK about ditching again, missy! You nearly gave me a nervous breakdown that time you forced me to cut girls chorus with you!"

Ignoring my vice-like grip, squaring her shoulders, and taking on a haughty expression, Lulu smugly replied, "Force you! I seem to remember you went with me of your own free will, Trixie. I don't remember any gun being pointed at your head."

True, there hadn't been any actual deadly weapons involved, but Lulu's powers of persuasion, innocent doe eyes, and the promise of a free banana split for me if I'd accompany her, were equally perilous. Tightening my hold on her arm, I firmly said to little miss smarty pants, "That's neither here nor there. Point is, you're not going into that joint now and that's final! Now march yourself over there with the other girls, before I -----"

I didn't get a chance to finish my threat, because Miss Corey showed up behind us and told us to get the lead out. I wasn't quite sure what that meant, but after she stabbed me in the back with an archery arrow, I figured it out.

Then, one fine day, the blue-haired Miss Corey announced that we were going to have a tournament to determine who the best bowler was. I already knew, but it seemed several stubborn people needed more proof than my flapping gums. I was positive I'd be able to bowl my usual 300, unless some dire circumstance reared its ugly head, as had happened to me in the past. I will confess that one time I bowled a measly 289, but that was only because my right arm, my bowling arm, was in a sling. I'd broken it the day before, while attempting a double wheelie on my bike. The reason it was only in a sling, instead of in a cast as I would have prescribed, was my mother, along with that quack of a Doctor Payne, insisted it wasn't broken. They both ignorantly claimed, "There's just some scraping on the elbow, Trixie." Humph! I'm of the firm belief that people who are sagely in touch with their own bodies, as I've always been, know instinctively when they've broken a bone.

Anyway, THIS time, there was nothing holding me back. No broken arms, and certainly no obnoxious boyfriends to make me nervous or otherwise distract me. It was no wonder some of my friends, like Margie and Bonita, were crummy bowlers. Who could concentrate with all that guy gawking!

But to tell the truth, the main reason I wanted to win the tournament was so I could get my mitts on that swell trophy the school was handing out! I'm pretty sure it was made of solid gold! It sure looked like it!

Competition day rolled around before we knew it and the Purdy Lanes was packed to the rafters. Every kid at PHS crowded into the bowling alley to witness the great event - and probably yours truly. Many of my friends were competing: Lulu, Margie, Bonita, Sugar, Kitty, and of course Dottie, since her dad owned the place. Most people thought Dottie would cream us all, since she was able to practice every day to her heart's content, not ever paying one red cent, but I knew, deep down inside, I was the one destined to win the gold trophy. Even though I was set to bowl another perfect game, I will admit all the girls were bowling okay, which was a really good thing, because you'd hate to make a fool of yourself, especially with the whole school watching! High school can be hard enough, without the added pressure of embarrassing yourself in front of a whole bunch of gossipy teenagers. I was so glad nothing like that had ever happened to me!

So . . . let the games begin! The skirmish was underway! Strike after strike; pins flying and mixing; crowd chanting TRIX-EE, TRIX-EE! It was coming down to the last frame. As every spectator waited with bated breath to watch the emerald green-eyed bowler finish off the game with a perfect 300, I picked up my pink ball with my handpainted yellow daisies, took dead aim at the pins, three-stepped down the alley with a perfect backswing, unleashed my powerful follow through, and ----- SPLAT!

Yes, I said SPLAT! I found myself catapulted halfway down the slippery alley. There I was facedown, squinting at nothing but polished wood, and spitting lane oil out of my mouth!

"What happened?" shrieked everyone, who hadn't been

left totally speechless. "How could such a disaster have occurred to the best bowler at Purdy High?"

When I finally came to my senses, I realized what had befallen me ----- my fingers had gotten stuck inside the holes of my bowling ball! Someone had sabotaged my ball by shoving chewed-up Bazooka bubble gum into the holes, thereby preventing my fingers from releasing said ball! Diabolical! Who could have done such a dastardly deed?

There were many possible suspects, but two names came to the forefront: Hubert Button and Ralphie Tittsworth! For some reason they were still holding a grudge against me for that boys locker room incident.

In an effort to do some investigative work just like Trixie Belden, the girl detective named after me, or so I assume, I approached each suspect separately and very casually asked, "May I please have a stick of gum?"

Ralphie replied, "I don't chew gum. Only tobacco and black licorice." Conclusion: Innocent!

Then I put the same question to Hubert. "Sure," he answered, handing me a small, wrapped square. "Have a Bazooka."

Aha! Proof positive! Forensic evidence! Plus it was the same shade of pink and gooey texture as that sinister concoction that nearly conked me out!

Hubert, of course, consistently denied being the culprit, despite practically being caught in the act. Since there were no other tests that could be given to settle conclusively who that gum belonged to, there was nothing more I could do at this point. My only recourse was to give him REAL dirty looks every time I saw him at school. I even practiced for hours in my bedroom mirror to come up with the crabbiest looks imaginable! Unfortunately, Hubert seemed completely unfazed by my scowly faces and even took to laughing every time I made one. Chalk up one more unpunished crime, with no closure for the victim!

Obviously I didn't bowl my usual 300 and Dottie Darlin, quite ruthlessly, snatched the victory from me. I logically suggested a do-over, since the ball hadn't left my hand until the second bounce, but Miss Corey unfairly denied my request. However, truth be told, I didn't care all that much. What I REALLY wanted was that trophy! Pondering my situation, I came up with a great solution! If I couldn't have the pure gold one from the school, I figured I could trot on over to the five-and-dime and buy myself a similar one with my babysitting money.

Hidden among the sundry items, on a dusty shelf way in the back of the store, I found exactly what I was looking for: a slightly-nicked, gold trophy with a little, white bowling pin on top. At $1.99, it was barely within my price range; nevertheless, I decided to splurge on the engraving, for a quarter more. Not bad! And I went all out: TRIXIE POOR - BEST BOWLER IN PHS HISTORY. That taken care of, life once again made sense.

The only unfinished business was the treacherous gum problem. As a result of my grueling experience, I was instrumental in forcing the Purdy School Board to ban all types of chewing gum, especially Bazooka, from future PHS bowling tournaments. It may have been too late for me, but I was determined to alleviate the suffering of future high school bowlers. You're welcome, Purdy High!

# DRIVING PURDY CRAZY

I was known for many things around good ol' Purdy High, but the one thing that has never been matched is this: I'm the only person, male or female, in PHS history to have taken drivers education twice! The first time I drove into a fairly small canyon rendering my teacher, Coach Cole Goodman, helpless and nearly comatose. I was immediately, in fact that very day, booted back to Miss Corey's P.E. class and told I would not be able to take drivers ed again until Coach fully recovered from the first bout of lessons. It took a few weeks, but one day a grinning Miss Corey exclaimed that I was "going to be somebody else's problem" (whatever that was supposed to mean) and the next day I was put in the driving class again.

My new partner was Dottie Darlin, the same Dottie Darlin whose dad owned the Purdy Bowling Lanes, the best bowling alley in town. Actually it was the ONLY bowling alley in town, but who cares? It was still the best. I liked the lanes okay, but Dottie was a different story.

I'd had a bone to pick with that little gal ever since she stole the solid gold bowling trophy from me. But I tried to forget about that injustice because I now had new worries concerning Miss Darlin. I was crossing my fingers that she wouldn't turn out to be a nervous Nelly like my first partner, Nelly Pumnut.

Dottie never struck me as the jittery type, yet you never know. I've heard of people getting pretty worked up when they're on the verge of going full blast down a mountain. I was so terrified of having another hysterical partner that I came right out and asked Dottie if she was prone to hysterics. I said in plain English, just like this. I said, "Dottie, are you going to have a cow when I get behind the wheel?" and she calmly replied, "No, Trixie, nothing you ever do flusters me." There. Later I was to learn that Dottie was a big, fat fibber!

The first thing Coach had us do with the car was stop and start at the top of Curley Hill, in front of the Moose Theater. This hill, according to my geometry calculations, was at a 90 degree angle. Of course the car had a clutch, which made for some grueling stops and starts. Some people, including Coach Goodman, might have said that Dottie was doing better than little ol' me in the driving department, but was it really fair to judge us equally? I think not. Dottie had her slightly older brother, Dickie, to give her extra lessons. The only sibling I had was Queenie, my German Shepherd, who'd told me repeatedly she'd rather give up her bones than help me drive. Ha! That's a little joke. Queenie couldn't really talk in a human voice.

As soon as Dottie was finished showing off, Coach told her to pull over to the side of the road and let me take the wheel. In a slightly shaky voice, Coach said, "Okay, Trixie, your turn. Do you think you can do the starts and stops without killing all of us?"

"I can't make any promises," I enthusiastically replied, "but I'll give it the ol' college try!"

"I guess that's about all I can ask for," he glumly said. "And if at all possible, please try not to strip the gears."

"Oh, Mr. Goodman, you're such a worry wart!" And with that I managed to strip the gears and stall the car smack dab in the middle of Curley Hill. When the car began rolling backward down the hill, Coach abruptly slammed on his set of brakes which were located on the side he'd been relegated to. I named these extra brakes "cheaters' brakes" and was extremely offended he'd felt the need to use them with me.

"I've had enough of this for one day," Coach blubbered, sweat streaming down his face. "Let's see if you can learn how to change a tire."

Dottie, the obvious teacher's pet, was again asked to drive us outside of town so we could learn how to change a tire. Coach took off one of the tires and began doing all the boring things you do when you're changing it: getting out the jack and spare tire from the trunk; putting the screws in the hubcap; taking the tire off; putting the new tire on . . . blah, blah, blah. Oh, I could hardly stand it! To be perfectly honest, I wasn't paying one teensy-weensy bit of attention. I knew, deep down inside, I would never, ever, in my whole entire life, change a tire. I would somehow find somebody else to do it, or I would simply drive it flat. After all, really, how much damage could that do? I'd still have three good tires to drive on and, if you ask me, four is simply overkill. But I plastered a very serious expression on my mug, furrowed my brow with all my might, and slowly nodded to confirm my understanding. Then I told Coach I'd seen enough, that watching Dottie do it so well was all I needed.

Coach looked at his Timex, decided we needed to stop our lesson for the day, and told Dottie to drive us back to Purdy High. Again, Dottie! Honestly, I was getting darn sick and tired of her and her showing off! And trophy stealing!

The next day Dottie and I took turns driving around Purdy. The only criticism Coach had for me was when he said, "Trixie, could you PLEASE shift to second gear so we can go more than five miles an hour?"

I did as instructed, but I really didn't see the point. If I wanted to go faster, all I needed to do was step on the gas. All this changing-gear business seemed like a huge waste of time, not to mention the fact that it was overworking the poor car. But I shifted gears anyway, just to keep Coach happy and to make him like me. Quite frankly, I was hoping to take over as teacher's pet!

Driving all over Purdy, from cruising down Curley Street, to passing my house on Fairgrounds Avenue, to swinging by Dottie's fancy house on Park Avenue, was turning out to be a lot of fun! Neither of us had succumbed to even ONE accident! Showing such good driving skills, we were informed by our teacher that we were ready to tackle Switchback Mountain, that two-lane winding road with sheer drop-offs. Dottie looked a little scared with no Dickie to hold her hand, but I was rarin' to go! My chance to prove to Coach Goodman, once and for all, what a swell driver I was!

The big day arrived, a little on the chilly side, but we were determined to face Switchback Mountain. Since I was going to be the first driver of the day, Coach told me to let the car warm up. I turned on the ignition and decided to tell him (and selfish Dottie) about my previous evening while we waited. I'm always good at providing delightful entertainment in a pinch.

"Well, Coach, for dinner we ate pork chops, mashed potatoes and creamed corn. I usually have half a Skippy peanut butter sandwich, a bag of Fritos, and a Snickers candy bar for my sack lunch, but I never have that for dinner, because it's not as nutritious and then, after helping my mom do the dishes, and giving Queenie her Alpo, I went to my room to do my homework, but I didn't really do any homework, because I wrote a letter to my French pen-pal instead, and then I came out of my room and watched I Love Lucy on the television set, which was so funny with Ethel and -----"

"Okay, Trixie, I think the car's warmed up enough so you -----"

"But wait, Coach! I didn't tell you the best part. I studied my drivers manual forward and back and I even memorized a lot of it!" Glancing over my shoulder to Dottie, I glowered, "Did YOU memorize the manual, Dottie?"

Dottie ignored me and continued chewing on a fingernail.

Humph! "Would you like to hear the manual backward, Coach?" Before he could answer I continued, "signals turn the use always." Then I quickly said into the rearview mirror, "I'll bet YOU can't do that, Dottie."

Before Dottie could show her ignorance by answering, Coach interrupted, "That's enough, Trixie. Release the emergency brake and let's get going."

"Emergency brake?! What emergency?! I didn't know there'd been an emergency!" I was frantic with questions.

Coach rolled his eyes, reached over and released the brake, then began breathing into the paper bag he always kept in the glove compartment. After a couple of minutes, he ordered me to drive.

Adjusting the rearview mirror so I could watch myself driving, I felt more than competent to head for Switchback Mountain. As we were leaving the school grounds, the boys track team came jogging along and what did Dottie do? Spotting her hunky brother, she quickly shoved her head out my window and began hollering, "Dickie! Dickie!" What an immature display! She was exhibiting no self-control whatsoever.

Since I wanted that good-looking jock to notice me too ---- I'd had a crush on him since fifth grade ---- I stuck my head out that same window, as far as my neck would allow, and yelled at the top of my lungs, "Hey, Dickie! Can't you run any faster than that, you big gooney bird?!"

The much sought-after Dickie caught sight of me and began running as if his shorts were on fire, in the opposite direction. I had to really burn rubber to try and catch up with him, but he took off so fast across the football field that he made a swift getaway! Rats! Lost another one.

With Dickie out of reach, I set my sights on the other cute guys in their gym shorts. Continuing to stretch my noggin out the car window as far as was humanly possible, while persistently honking the horn to get their attention, I began shouting as loud as a howler monkey: "Hey Hubert, Ralphie, look at me! Barney, Billy, it's me, Trixie! I'm driving! Look at me!" Honk. Honk.

As they scrambled to get out of the way, the car suddenly veered toward a good-sized ditch. Right away I thought, "Oh brother! Here we go again ----" but Coach pulled the wheel back, just in the nick of time. The pale, perspiring teacher muttered something about "hazard pay" then pointed down the road with a trembling finger while managing to croak, "Trixie, drive toward Switchback Mountain and stop chasing the boys, for crying out loud."

"Yes, sir!" Ready or not, Switchback Mountain, here I come!

It was a warm sunny morning, perfect for a leisurely

drive. The birds were singing, the fresh mountain air smelled of pine trees, all was mellow and right with the world. Then it happened! From out of nowhere a huge, roly-poly squirrel appeared in the middle of the road, right where my left wheels were aimed! Oh, no! What could I do? I couldn't run over a SQUIRREL, Purdy High's mascot! So I did the only thing any good Purdy High Squirrel would do ---- I quickly swerved to the right, careened down a long embankment at fifty miles an hour, and crashed into a cluster of juniper trees!

Well, once Dottie's screams had subsided and Coach had untwined himself from the fetal position, I decided to wander back up the hill and check on my squirrel. Not only did I want to take a gander at my squirrel, but I had to get away from Dottie's obnoxious and quite unnecessary shrieks. Those bleats were really starting to get on my nerves. I distinctly remember her saying she wouldn't act up like Nelly if I had a minor fender bender. And now look at her! What a little storyteller!

When I finally reached the top of the ravine, after picking a few yellow daisies along the way to give to Coach Goodman, there sat Mr. Squirrel himself, smug as could be. He was positioned right in the middle of the road, smirking as if he owned it. When I tried to approach him to give him a little pat, he snarled menacingly and acted like he was going to bite my hand off! Ingrate! Brat! I'd always heard that squirrels, members of the rodent family, didn't make very good pets and now I believed it. I vowed never again to beg my folks to buy me a squirrel for my birthday.

Long story short, everyone in Purdy agreed I'd acted very heroically in saving that squirrel's life. Well, maybe not Coach Goodman and Dottie. But there were rumors swirling around that there should be a parade in my honor. Unfortunately, the committee couldn't find that squirrel to sit on a float with me, so the parade was out. I had to settle for a certificate of thanks and a special school assembly, which was okay with me. And the certificate was dandy! It was handwritten in pencil on a sheet of yellow, lined paper and read as follows: "Thanks Trixie POO." As anyone with two peepers can see, the R was inadvertently left off. Not wanting to make a federal case out of it, I merely took my red pen and wrote in a fat R. I also thought the commendation needed some punching up so I added, again in red, the word "undying" at the beginning and "every Squirrel's friend" at the end. It looked fine after that.

Mr. Fuffenhoff, the Principal of PHS, had the prestigious honor of handing over my precious certificate during the assembly, along with a huge bouquet of yellow daisies. According to the Purdy Evening Courier, which wrote a lengthy article on my ceremony, seated on the stage were the following: Mr. Rizzo, our assistant principal; Mr. Floyd Toot, the Mayor of Purdy; Mr. Kurt Langley, Purdy's Chief of Police; as well as many other dignitaries from around the state. I was informed that Coach Goodman had also been invited to honor me, but once again he was on a little vacation. What a coincidence that those vacations always occurred right after I'd been in his drivers ed class.

Anyway, enough about Coach Goodman and his vacations and back to me. As I was being presented with my fabulous certificate, the audience spontaneously erupted into wild cheers! The cheers were followed by chanting: "Speech, Trixie! Speech!"

I didn't hear those words very often, in fact never, so I was completely taken aback. Usually what I heard was, "Be quiet, Trixie! Be quiet!" People wanting me to open my mouth was such an unusual request I hardly knew how to respond! Once over the initial shock, however, I was able to give the admirers what they wanted. Raising my arms to calm down my fans, I cleared my throat a couple of times, then went into my eloquent two-hour speech. I thanked everyone I could think of, from the highway department for building the road on Switchback Mountain, to the painters who painted lines on it.

When I finished with my little talk, the house lights came on and I was finally able to look out at my supporters. From my vantage point I witnessed the sweetest thing. All these adoring people, onstage and in the audience, had their eyes closed in what I can only assume were prayers of thanks to me. Oh, my! Wanting to reciprocate their heartfelt gesture, I folded my hands over my heart, closed my eyes, and solemnly replied, "You're welcome, Purdy High!"

# POTLUCKS AND
# SQUIRRELETTES

It was Easter break in 1964 and I was a junior at good ol'
PHS. Although I belonged to many school organizations,
one of my favorites was the Squirrelettes, the girls pep
club. The main goal of this group was to promote school
spirit in many different ways. Besides sitting together at
football games in a special cheering section, we decorated
the halls on game day, sold programs and pins to raise
money, festooned goal posts with blue and gold crepe
paper and wore the blue and gold school colors on color
day. There was even a rooter bus that took us to out-of-
town games such as were held in Podunk and Furnace
City.

The Squirrelettes also sponsored potlucks to thank the
athletes and faculty for their hard work and dedication to
Purdy High. This Spring we decided to have the potluck at
the Lookout Mountain picnic grounds, located at the base
of the mountain. Since it was Easter break, I thought it

would be fun to include an Easter egg hunt. I dyed several dozen eggs and bought some small chocolate bunny rabbits wrapped in gold foil, then hid them all along the Lookout Mountain trails the day before the picnic. I'd spent my own babysitting money on those eggs and rabbits so I asked Mrs. Weems, the English teacher/Squirrelettes sponsor, if I could have some moolah to reimburse myself. I was well aware that each girl who joined the Squirrelettes was obligated to pay a twenty-five cent initiation fee, so I knew darn good and well the club was loaded. Mrs. Weems said she'd make sure I got two dollars compensation. It didn't quite cover my expenses but, being an overly-generous person, I decided to let the nickel slide.

The day of the potluck looked beautiful. Not a cloud in the sky. Even the KNUT 97.3 disc jockey was predicting perfect weather. That was good news, if you believed it, but I knew better. The previous year I'd been Purdy High's school mascot, Squirrely Squirrel, which was considered a great honor by at least one emerald green-eyed person. I'm not positive if anyone else considered it a great honor, but I didn't care. Wearing the brown jumpsuit and paper machier head that resembled any number of animals, I performed at all the different games, instilling enthusiasm in the fans by jumping around and clapping my paws, even though I couldn't see a blasted thing with that head on. Sometimes the football players would get mad if I somehow wandered onto the field when they were on the ten-yard line, and a couple of times the cheerleaders threatened to tie me up and leave me in the locker room, claiming I was "always in the way." Anyway, during one particularly perilous and death-defying doozy of a somersault, I'd rolled too far to the right and twisted my back. After receiving that nearly debilitating sports injury, which almost forced me to give up the squirrel gig, my lumbago could always predict if rain was in the forecast.

Knowing my lumbago was never wrong, I approached the Squirrelettes officers and Mrs. Weems in the PHS parking lot and tried to warn them of the impending rain. They simply shook their heads and pooh-poohed me, as they were prone to do. "Oh, Trixie, you and your stupid lumbago! Do you really think your dumb back knows more than the weatherman at KNUT?"

"I most certainly do," I replied, using the most indignant voice I could come up with. "Wasn't I right about it raining last weekend?"

"Well, yes, you were, but every single weatherman on radio and TV was predicting that rain. I hardly think your 'clairvoyant' back did anything so great," said Dottie Darlin, in an exceedingly snippy tone.

"Fine! Go ahead and have your potluck today, but don't say I didn't warn you!" Uttering those final words of admonition, I packed up the grub, aided by the other Squirrelettes and lettermen, and we all set out for the picnic grounds.

As soon as the chow was unloaded, all the kids, followed by the faculty members, scattered to begin searching for the eggs and bunnies that I'd hidden the day before. The jocks, especially Dickie Darlin, were particularly enthusiastic. Of course, being the hardest worker I ever knew, I stayed behind to start laying out the food and accoutrements. That's French for "other stuff" I think. After half an hour everyone was finding lots of eggs, but no chocolate bunnies.

"Are you sure you hid those chocolates, Trixie? All we can find are little wadded up pieces of gold foil littered about!" yelled several girls, including itty-bitty Lulu Dilly, who could sniff out chocolate from a mile away and was known for having a fondness for anything chocolate, especially those hot fudge sundaes at the Gulp n Gobble.

"Oh, well . . ." I thought to myself, "I may have accidentally eaten a few ---- like all but one!" Then aloud I hollered back, "Just keep looking! You're bound to find them sooner or later!" (Yeah, if a chipmunk doesn't find it first.) "Stop bothering me! I have to get these tables set up!"

To tell the truth, I already had everything all laid out, but I wanted to examine the scarred picnic tables more carefully. Nearly every wooden table on the grounds was full of knife marks. One of the most prevalent was "Cheery P+Gil S" gouged in big, bold letters on not only the tables, but half a dozen pine trees to boot! I was definitely going to have to take that knife away from Cheery! There were also quite a few "Trixie loves Mr. Richley" and "Trixie+BS" and "Trixie+RG" and "Trixie+AR," etc. Maybe I shouldn't have done all that but I was pretty sure no one would know

I'd been the culprit, since I'd cleverly left off the initial of my last name, not to mention my whole last name. Quite frankly, I couldn't even remember who some of those other initials associated with my first name belonged to, since I'd been leaving my mark for years. I was really starting to enjoy myself, trying to decipher the letters, when I heard, "Trixie, get over here and give us some hints." The loudest bellowing came from Winnie Ragsdale and Margie Sweetum. "Play Hot and Cold with us so we can find the bunnies!"

I had no desire to play Hot and Cold with a bunch of Squirrelettes and jocks, let alone Pop McNultie or Coach Goodman, but I knew they wouldn't leave me alone until I did. Wanting to have some peace so I could figure out who the many other initials belonged to, I hollered back, "You're all as cold as ice! Run to the top of Lookout Mountain and you'll be hot! And be sure and take your raincoats with you!" To that they just howled, "Raincoats! There's not a cloud in the sky, you nut!" Ignoring them, I returned to my studies . . . who could TS+SW be? And this DP+CA, and this ----?

All of a sudden the sky began to darken as ominous clouds rolled in from "P" Mountain. I knew immediately this spelled trouble and we were in for one heck of a downpour, just as my lumbago had so accurately predicted. Since everyone else was way up on top of Lookout Mountain searching for those illusive chocolate rodents, I dashed to my folks' reliable '49 Chevy, slipped into my raincoat and shower cap and retrieved the plastic tarps I'd so sensibly had the foresight to bring along. I quickly got the eats and tableware covered, just as the first few silver dollar-sized raindrops began to fall.

While I hunkered comfortably under one of the tables, dry as a bone and nibbling on tasty deviled eggs, the rest of the gang at last came stumbling down the hill, looking like drowned rats or, in this case, drowned squirrels. Even though the cloudburst had stopped as suddenly as it had begun, the damage was already done. The normally perfect hairdos of bubbles and flips, plastered into place with a can of Aqua Net hairspray, had transformed into wet, sticky, stringy mops.

"Why, oh why, didn't we listen to you, Trixie?" cried Kitty Shrub and Nellie Pumnut, trying to repair the messes on top of their noggins. "Your wise lumbago said it was going to rain, but we wouldn't pay attention. Now we're paying the price for our stubbornness."

The best I could offer were a few clucking sounds with my tongue and a tilt of my head.

"When will we ever learn that you know best and are always right?" wailed Ralphie Tittsworth, Davey Goodnuff and Dickie Darlin, shaking their heads like that pooch, Duke, from the Beverly Hillbillies. At least I THINK that's what they were saying. I'm not sure, because it was really hard to concentrate with that smell. One thing I am sure about was they stunk to high heaven! A mixture of wet wool and moth balls was emanating from their lettermen's sweaters, not to mention the unmistakable odor of hound dog.

Trying my best not to gag on their pungent smell, I merely nodded to acknowledge their lack of faith in me. Then I gracefully gestured to the tables, extending my right palm upward and outward in true Price is Right fashion, my mom's favorite daytime television show. I walked around the tables removing the tarps, unveiling a smorgasbord of sumptuous delicacies and allowing the disbelievers to witness with their own eyes how I'd saved their potluck from utter ruination. (And, might I add, being the humble person that I am, I never once said "I told you so" ---- even though I thought it more times than a nice person would care to admit.)

Barney Flume, the ever-present photographer for The Squirrely Times, captured a lovely shot of the potluck buffet and the next day the photo made it to the front page of The Purdy Evening Courier. After Barney's photo appeared in the newspaper, along with the stupendous article written by Mr. Nikniewicz praising me, word of my impressive lumbago spread like the common cold around PHS, as well as the entire town of Purdy. Organizations galore were calling me at home to find out what my extraordinary ailment was predicting for that day's weather. One man in particular called me every single morning around seven o'clock to get my prediction. He refused to give me his name, but I thought this mystery man sounded exactly like the KNUT weatherman. I obligingly gave everyone the forecast, thereby preventing many a potluck catastrophe, rummage sale drenching, garden tea party washout and picnic fiasco. It may not seem like a big deal to some, but if you've ever eaten a tuna casserole soaked in tepid rain water, you wouldn't scoff. Hundreds of activities were saved from being turned into soggy disappointments, thanks to me and my lumbago. You're welcome, Purdy!

# SAVING THE SPEECH TEAM

In the early Sixties, the Purdy School Board hired a new faculty member to teach speech classes at Purdy High. This new man's name was Mr. Beau Richley and, boy howdy, was he ever cute! He was so much younger and better looking than all our other old geezer teachers such as Pop McNultie, Mr. Snedley, Mr. Bunson or Coach Goodman. My chorus teacher, Mr. Campbell, was quite dapper, but not that young. I think he was pushing thirty.

Not only did Mr. Richley have the suave, movie star looks of the impressive Mr. Paul Newman, but he was a snazzy dresser to boot! He always wore well-fitting suits that clung to his hunky torso to a T. Then he'd expertly polish off his handsomeness with a colorful, skinny tie. Skinny ties looked so cool, not like those fat, ugly ties the old-timers wore to complement their cardigan sweaters buttoned halfway down the front. And if all this weren't heavenly enough, Mr. Richley smelled divine! The only cologne I'd ever recognized was Old Spice, which seemed to be the aroma of choice of most of the seasoned educators. My dad never wore cologne, preferring instead the fresh, clean scent of Ivory soap, which, amazingly enough, floated in water.

One time I got up the nerve to ask Mr. Richley what kind of cologne he was wearing and he amiably replied, "It's called English Leather. My girlfriend, who still lives in Furnace City, gave it to me for Christmas."

Humph! Girlfriend?! Furnace City! I'm surprised she doesn't live in Podunk, along with all the other squares! Anyway, I wrote down those words, English Leather, in my diary on the very same, memorable day Mr. Richley told them to me. I would never forget those words as long as I lived, especially now that they were etched in my special book for all eternity.

I had such a crush on Mr. Richley that I would have taken any class he taught (even geometry) to be able to stare at him and whiff his English Leather on a daily basis. When I found out he was going to be teaching speech classes, I was in hog heaven! A class where you were actually encouraged to speak, instead of always being told to shut up by the teacher or else you'd get sent to Mr. Rizzo's office, well, that was right up my alley! And if grades were determined by how MUCH you could talk in class, then I was sure to be the best and get an A++!

This new teacher, who everybody called Mr. Richley, but I called Mr. Dreamboat, started a speech club. Hot diggity dog! Count me in! Not only could I drool over

Mr. Dreamboat during my speech class, but I could continue the salivation after school as well! When we had to pick a category in which to compete with other schools, I immediately thought mine should be debate, since I could argue 'til I was blue in the face. If not that maybe extemporaneous, since I could yak 'til the cows came home about subjects I knew nothing about. But Mr. Richley didn't like either of those. What did he stick me in? Humorous! All I could think of at the time was he must have been short-handed in that category.

One fine morning, about five o'clock in the morning, the speech team piled onto a school bus and headed for Central High in the big metropolis of Furnace City. We'd slaughtered Central High during our homecoming football game in '61 with a score of 20-18, and I knew we'd cream them again in the speech tournament.

Usually Mr. Paprocki would drive us, which was okay by me, because Mr. Paprocki was the very nice bus driver on my daily school bus route. Today, however, there was no Mr. Paprocki, his absence being excused by the appearance of his brand new baby boy, so it was Mr. Dreamboat himself taking the wheel! Whoop-dee-doo! I hollered "Shotgun!" before anyone else, then, remembering there was no passenger seat, I settled in behind the driver's seat for two glorious hours of English Leather! Under normal circumstances I would have made the kids sing "Ninety-Nine Bottles of Beer on the Wall," but today was different. All I wanted to do was stare at the back of you-know-who's perfectly-shaped head and intoxicate myself with the scent of English Leather.

Knowing my beloved was securely confined behind the steering wheel, I surmised I could take advantage of the situation and engage Mr. Dreamboat in a bit of idle chit-chat. "Did you notice I put my hair up in a ponytail today, Mr. Richley?" I coyly asked. " I woke up five minutes early to do it."

"Yes, Trixie, I noticed but since you're competing in Humorous, I guess it'll be okay."

Swell! He likes it! I knew he would. "Did you notice the new penny loafers my mom bought for me?

"Uh-huh. Uh-huh."

"I think I might win a first-place trophy today."

"Uh-huh. Uh-huh."

"I think you should keep splashing English Leather on yourself and never switch to Old Spice."

"Uh-huh. Uh-huh."

Before we knew it we'd made it to Furnace City at a little after seven o'clock. It's so true what they say: there's nothing like a stimulating conversation to make the time go by quickly. When we got off the bus the temperature was at least 150 degrees, by my estimation. I didn't care for it myself, in fact I hated it, but everyone kept saying it was a "dry heat" so I guess there was something wrong with me and it really wasn't hot after all. Maybe my internal thermometer wasn't functioning properly. I'd go ask Mrs. Shott, the school nurse, on Monday.

The morning's competitions zipped by and every single PHS Squirrel advanced to the semi-finals. We didn't care about beating the schools in Furnace City so much, but we REALLY wanted to defeat the Podunk High Skunks, our biggest rival for everything. When the Purdy team met up in Central's cafeteria for lunch, Kitty, Lulu and I spotted the Podunk team standing over by the desserts. I really wanted to shout, "Podunk stinks!" and then hide behind the cafeteria ladies, but Mr. Dreamboat got wind of it and put a stop to it.

With that fun taken away from me, I figured I might as well pick out my lunch. We had two choices: a delicious cheeseburger with all the fixin's, or some creepy, little, comma-shaped things called "shrimps." Not only did those shrimps remind me of the horrible scorpions we always had to be careful of but they were really slimy, like melted Oleo margarine, or Clarence Waddle's hair after he put too much Brylcreem on it. Well, I knew I wasn't about to touch any of those shrimps, let alone EAT one, and neither was anyone else with a lick of sense. Those icky-looking things were way too raunchy for us Purdy kids, who'd never seen anything so disgusting in our lives. The only one who chose the shrimps, and I say this with deep disappointment, was the charming Mr. Richley. The fact that I didn't say Mr. Dreamboat is no mistake, if you get my drift. We all pigged out on our lunches, especially our teacher: "In Purdy I rarely have an opportunity to indulge in this delicacy," Mr. Dreamboat confided, after consuming at least a hundred of the gross little things. Yes, I said Dreamboat. I could never stay mad at him!

The afternoon semi-finals and finals went off without a hitch. Every Purdy High School Speech Team member made it to the finals, meaning that when we finally gathered in Central's auditorium at the end of the competition to find out who'd won the trophies and certificates, the PHS team was going crazy! Category after category we took first place: Stanley Weiss in Debate; Lulu Dilly in Oratory; Kitty Shrub in Serious Prose; Hubert Button in Extemporaneous ---- just to name a few. Oh, and yours truly in Humorous, which surprised me more than anyone. What a blast! We'd picked up more trophies and certificates than any other school! (Including, thank heaven, the stinky Podunk Skunks!)

Alas, the jubilant ceremonies being over with, it was time to get on the bus and drive the two hours back to good ol' Purdy. The delinquents, who wanted to neck all the way home in the dark, scrambled for the seats way in the back ---- you know who you are, Bonita Ruiz and Clarence Waddle! And Margery Sweetum and Billy Bunson! Despite my obvious maturity, I wasn't one of those delinquents, and wouldn't be for a few more years, so I set my sights on leading a rousing chorus of my favorite song ---- yes, "Ninety-Nine Bottles of Beer on the Wall." I'd just finished tapping my baton on Davey Goodnuff"'s noggin to get everyone's attention when, to my horror, a ghostly Mr. Dreamboat appeared at the open bus door. Moaning and clutching his stomach, he fell onto the steps and tried to pull himself up to the driver's seat. I rushed over to him, kneeled down beside his listless body, and begged to know what was wrong.

"The shrimps, Trixie, the shrimps! They poisoned me!" He grasped one of my hands with his two clammy ones and pleaded, "You've got to drive these kids home, Trixie! Drive, Trixie! Drive like the wind! Drive like you've never driven before! You were the best driver in Coach Goodman's drivers ed class, despite what Dottie Darlin said, and now you've got your REAL drivers license, not that crummy learners permit, where you can only drive if your mother's sitting in the front seat with you, so save the day and take my people home! I know it's a lot to ask, but I know you can do it! So drive, Trixie, and I'll see you later in Purdy, after I get my stomach pumped out. Oh, here's the ambulance now ----"

With those encouraging words echoing in my ears, I reluctantly quit holding hands with him and allowed the medics to cart him off. I didn't want to release his hands as they were so manly and strong ---- icy cold and wet, yet somehow strangely desirable. Duty called, however, and since he was already blacking out while being wheeled into the ambulance, I obediently got behind the wheel of the huge, yellow behemoth.

I'd never driven anything other than the drivers ed car and my parents' Sherman tank of a '49 Chevy, but I figured it couldn't be that hard. Turns out I was right! It was a piece of cake! As I barreled up the interstate headed toward Purdy, I performed several maneuvers to insure a safe trip: I honked the horn every mile to keep everyone informed of our progress; I turned on the windshield wipers every fifteen minutes, in the off chance it might rain; I flipped on the turn signals and poked the flashers at ten-minute intervals, just to make sure they were still working; and, perhaps most importantly of all, I slammed on the brakes every time the kids stopped singing "Ninety-Nine Bottles of Beer." With all those precautions in place, we made it to Purdy in record speed, under forty-five minutes, and I was able to return my charges safely to the Purdy High parking lot.

For some unfathomable reason there were a few nervous Nellies sitting in the front who'd fainted along the way. Nelly Pumnut was among them, but then that should come as no surprise. I remember how flustered she'd been when she was lucky enough to be my drivers ed partner. The other fainters had, no doubt, been subjected to way too much of that Furnace City heat. I'd heard a lot of shrieking from hysterical backseat drivers, among them Ralphie Tittsworth and Davey Goodnuff. They were getting on my nerves so much that I finally had to stand up, steer the wheel with my left foot, then turn around to look them straight in their beady little eyes and yell, "Keep your big fat traps shut!" After all, I'd missed that coyote by a good inch and a half, and nobody but a cat could have seen that skunk in the dark, and you'd think that scatterbrained deer could have seen the bus driving straight toward him. By the way, those critters can jump a lot higher than you'd think! But, on the whole, you never saw a happier bunch of kids get off a bus! Some of them even kissed the ground!

So there you have it ---- the complete story of how I saved a whole busload of PHS speech team members from having to spend the rest of the school year in Furnace City. You're welcome, Purdy High!

# HAIR-RAISING HAVOC

Besides babysitting to earn an extra buck or two, I had a swell after-school job. I worked at La Belle Beauty Shop on Muller Road, right next door to the KNUT 97.3 radio station, Purdy's best, and only, radio station. The same station where I'd had my brief, but illustrious, stint as a disc jockey. I wasn't technically a "beautician," but sweeping up hair, disinfecting combs and brushes, mopping the floor and scrubbing the toilet every day after closing provided me with a great deal of knowledge about hair. If Sissy Applebaum, the attractive, young, shop owner and beautician, could cut, dye, perm and style hair, why couldn't I?

I pondered and pondered that question. What did Sissy have that I didn't? Well, maybe a few months at that beauty college right down the road and a few more years of experience, but other than that . . . So I figured I could do all that fancy stuff to hair without batting an eyelash. Really, if truth be told, how hard could it be? After all, it wasn't brain surgery. Speaking of brain surgery . . . hmm . . . I could probably do that, too, if equipped with a sharp butcher knife and ball-peen hammer. Anyway, I told three of my buddies to meet me at the shop after hours and to be prepared for the hair makeover of their lives! I would doll them up for the upcoming school play tryouts, which they were all interested in. For a small fee, of course: a quarter for the basic shampoo and set; fifty cents for the whole shebang, meaning cut, dye job and perm.

My guinea pigs . . . er, I mean . . . clients were Margery Sweetum, Sugar Wiggins and Bonita Ruiz. They showed up one evening around six o'clock, just as I was changing into my "work top." My work top was actually an old blouse left over from my elementary school days, but since I hadn't grown any in the last few years, it still fit me perfectly. The only thing wrong with it were the stains on the front from Queenie slobbering all over it, and some whitewash that had appeared out of nowhere. I considered myself quite fortunate that, as a high schooler, I could still fit into my clothes from the fourth grade. I knew some poor creatures who had to buy blouses every six months, because they kept growing out of them. One time I wore a new dress to school that Winnie Ragsdale swore looked exactly like the one she used to own, complete with the mismatched button on the front. When I got home I asked my mom where she'd bought the frock and she honestly replied, "The rummage sale at the Episcopalian Church. I got it for a quarter. Did you notice how the emerald green color matches your eyes?" Hmm . . . maybe it had been Winnie's. Well, too bad; it was mine now. Besides, there's no way it would fit Winnie anymore. Anyway, Margie, Sugar and Bonita, three kids who had that same terrible growing problem as Winnie, were very excited to find out what I could do for their mops.

Margie was the first to request my assistance, since she would be trying out for the lead in The Rat that Roared. "I need a new look, Trixie. I'm thinking of going for a Flip. You know Gidget looks absolutely adorable in hers. What do you think?" I liked Flips okay even though I, myself, sported the popular Bubble. I found Bubbles to be far more mature-looking and, yes, downright sophisticated. They were smooth and sleek and had an air of royalty about them. Just look at Audrey Hepburn's shiny do! Most of the famous Hollywood ingenues and starlets, such as Annette Funicello and Sandra Dee, had ravishing Bubbles. There were many other reasons, too numerous to mention, why I preferred the Bubble over the Flip, but the most important one, the one that I almost forgot, was this: I could never get my hair to go in a Flip. The only drawback to a Bubble was it gave spiders a place to hide.

"Take a seat, Margie Girl! I'm going to face you away from the mirror so that when the big reveal comes, you'll be ecstatically thrilled." Margie obediently plopped down in the barber chair, draping the plastic cape over herself, while I retrieved my cuticle scissors from the back pocket of my pink and white striped pedal-pushers. Then I merrily began snipping away, all the while crooning "Moon River" in my melodious, and definitely loud, voice.

"Do you have to do that right in my ear, Trixie?" squawked Margie, reaffirming just how fussy she could be.

Humph! As wads of Margie's hair cascaded down to the floor, I knew I was onto something. Perhaps I'd found my calling and was destined to become a famous beauty operator to the stars. I could do the hair of all the beautiful movie stars ---- maybe even the guys ---- like James Garner, one of the cutest actors I'd ever laid my emerald green eyes on. I think I was starting to drool.

"Oh my gosh, Trixie! Stop daydreaming and pay attention to what you're doing!"

"I AM paying attention, Margery." Actually, I wasn't, but I didn't need her any madder at me than she already was. "Let me just finish up a couple of little sections here ----" Oh, dear. I didn't think those bald spots in the back should have been there. I tried covering them up, by yanking down the long hair growing out of the top of her head.

"Stop it! You're pulling my hair out!" yelled Margie, overreacting as usual.

"Simmer down, Margie. Oh, no! Look what you made me do!" I thought maybe that would work.

"Made you do? Just let me see what you've done and then get me out of here!" shrieked the overwrought overreactor.

I ever so slowly turned the barber chair back toward the mirror, ready to receive all the praise I so richly deserved, when Margie suddenly caught sight of herself. Stunned for a split second, she then let out a scream! "Trixie, what in the blazes have you done to my hair?! It doesn't look like a flip ---- it looks like a big, fat FLOP!"

Well, you can imagine how crushed I was, not to mention shaky, since she'd scared me half to death with that unnecessary screech of hers! For a moment I was afraid I was being attacked by an owl. I thought Margie's hair looked really neat, as did Sugar and Bonita, judging by the huge grins on their faces. But then, without even bothering to say thank-you, Margie bolted from the chair, ripped off the cape and ran out the door!

"But what about my half dollar ---- ?" I wailed. She was already long gone.

Next was Sugar's turn but, for some reason, she seemed reluctant to sit in the barber chair. "Sugar, I've been advising Miss Corey on her rinse color ever since we started high school," I said reassuringly. "I think that midnight blue color would look ravishing with your complexion. That's my professional opinion, you see."

"Oh, I don't think so, Trixie. It looks nifty on Miss Corey, but I was thinking more along the lines of a few luxurious auburn highlights. Auburn is so rich-looking."

Wanting to be agreeable, and not wanting to look like a dumb bunny who didn't know what "auburn" meant, I replied, "Ten-four! Let's go with auburn!"

Well, to be perfectly honest, I thought "auburn" meant "orange." Cut to the chase, Sugar was not happy with the final result. She whooped and hollered and, quite frankly, made herself look even scarier than she already did with that orange hair.

"Now I'll never get a part in The Rat that Roared," she cried. "Maybe a Howdy Doody or Red Skelton look-alike contest, but that's it! Thanks a LOT, Trixie!"

With those loud words of thanks echoing throughout the shop, Sugar leaped from the chair, tore off her cape and charged out the door. I still didn't receive the twenty-five cents . . . uh, make that fifty cents . . . coming to me, however I did at least get a thank-you.

As I was watching Sugar race out the front door, from the corner of my eye I noticed Bonita inching her way toward the same door. "Where are you going, Bonita? We haven't given you your perm yet," I reminded her.

"Uh, it's okay, Trixie. My hair's curly enough," stammered a very pale Bonita.

"No, it isn't! Look, kiddo, if you want to get a part in that play, we need to give you a perm. I heard you want the role of the beauty queen. Well, let me tell you something. A lot of girls could try out for that part, including myself. In fact, I have the same measurements as you ---- just in a different order ---- so if you want to beat out your competition, you'll need to give it your all. Now, put this mask on and sit down in that chair while I mix up the somewhat toxic, yet not quite lethal, permanent wave solution."

Well, Bonita landed in the chair, but it appeared to have been more from fainting, rather than sitting. As a matter of fact, my rather uncooperative client was out cold the entire time she was getting the perm. I hate to say this, but it made my job a whole lot easier. Dealing with hard-to-please prima donnas was no picnic and I was beginning to rethink my ambition of becoming a famous beautician to the stars. I was thinking of going back to my other career goals: first woman President of the United States, or warden in a women's penitentiary. Every single member of my family and all but one of my friends said I'd be a shoo-in for the latter.

As I was spraying the last can (total five) of Aqua Net Extra Super Hold on Bonita's hair, she started to come around. "Where am I?" she asked groggily. "I had the most terrible nightmare . . . I was in some beauty parlor and this demented lunatic, who looked a lot like you, Trixie, had given me a perm and . . . whaaat the ----?!" Bonita caught a glimpse of herself in the large mirror. "It wasn't a horrible dream! It's real life! And YOU are the demented lunatic, Trixie! I might have known . . . uh, you . . . you . . . !"

Bonita carried on like that for a good half hour. The crazy way she was acting, you'd have thought someone had set her hair on fire . . . which, actually, I did . . . just a little bit . . . but not ALL her hair. There remained two small patches that weren't singed. But did Bonita care about THAT? No! All Miss Negative could focus on was the frizz ---- and three or four shiny spots showing bare scalp. I calmly tried to interject some logic into her rant: "Bonita, dear, with a bad attitude, such as the one you're displaying at this moment, you're never going to achieve your goal of portraying the beauty queen in our most prestigious school play. Nothing is to be gained by pointing nasty fingers at someone who is unselfishly dedicating her time to ----"

My pep talk was cut short as a large bottle of White Rain shampoo came whizzing by my right ear, slightly grazing my temple. "Can it, you little kook! I'll win a part in the play all right, if what they're looking for is a Harpo Marx twin!" yelled Bonita, the hurler of the projectile.

I don't know why she felt the need to holler; I was standing right there. Then, just like those other two ingrates, she jumped from the chair, yanked off her cape and fled out the door. "And my fifty cents? I'll settle for a quarter," I pleaded to her fleeing back.

"You'll get your quarter when Furnace City freezes over," she snottily replied as the door banged shut. Again, no words of thanks for me.

Over the next couple of weeks, my life wasn't quite as cool as it normally was. Those three ungrateful people told everyone in Purdy High, as well as anyone in the town of Purdy who owned a set of ears, that "Trixie ruined my hair." Ruined? What an exaggeration! I might agree with the word "different," but "ruined?" In my professional beauty operator's opinion, orange, fuzzy, choppy hair is not ruined. It's simply different. Besides, Margie had the added benefit of becoming quite proficient at doing handsome comb-overs, just like the old geezers at school who were at least forty! Not only were the three stooges slandering me, but they were telling all the boys in school not to ask me out on a date. Ha! Since that never happened anyway, it didn't bother me in the least. You'll have to think of some other way to punish me, girls!

Eventually everything got resolved, as things tend to do in life. (Sometimes I amaze myself at my advanced level of maturity and wisdom.) The girls' hair went back to the same ol' dumb, boring way it had been before I got my paws on it and Margie, Sugar and Bonita all got leading parts in The Rat that Roared. SEE! And you three crybaby ninnies said I ruined your hair! So even though you never did say thank-you, except for Sugar, and you never did pay me the fifty cents apiece you owed me ---- let alone give me a tip! ---- I'll still say you're welcome. And since I firmly believe my unique hairstyles gave the girls their motivation to try out for the play, I will also take credit for making The Rat that Roared a resounding success. You're welcome, Purdy High!

# CRISIS AT THE CHRISTMAS HOP

It was that special time of year and I wanted to attend the Purdy High School Christmas Hop. Once again I didn't have a date, and once again I didn't care! I planned on going to that doggone dance one way or another! However, I was facing some obstacles.

The official dance committee consisted of Margery Sweetum, Lulu Dilly, Hubert Button, and Ralphie Tittsworth. Unfortunately for me, Dottie Darlin was not only part of the group, but its leader to boot. Dottie, like my French teacher, Mrs. Snotgrass, had it in for me. She said, "As head of this committee, I hereby proclaim that Trixie be banned from the hop, unless she can somehow, miraculously, scrounge up a date. Last year, when I went to the dance with Gil Snedley because Cheery was out of town, Trixie made a big, fat pest of herself! She poked her dumb head in between Gil and me when Barney Flume was trying to take our photo. She said it was to "enhance" it. And then she kept cutting in on our dances. It was bad enough she kept horning in on us, but then she'd have the gall to give us dancing lessons ---- right there on the dance floor! Like she's such a great hoofer! She can barely walk in a straight line without falling flat on her face!"

Ha! Dottie was so lame, she didn't even know I'd done all those things intentionally. How DARE she go out with my good friend's boyfriend! Cheery heard about my sabotage and thanked me by doing my geometry homework for a month! That'll teach Dottie to mess with people's boyfriends!

Luckily for me, my best friend was also on the committee, so Margie attempted to come to my defense. "Oh, Trixie's not so bad. The only thing that made me a little mad last year was when she sat down at our table, practically on Billy Bunson's lap, and started slobbering in our lime sherbet punch because she was too lazy to go fetch her own. But other than that ----"

The committee had heard enough. All the students, except Margie, were in agreement that I should be banned. Even the teacher sponsors ---- Pop McNultie, Coach Goodman, and Mr. Peabody ---- considered me, to use their unflattering word, a menace. Miss Corey and Mrs. Lafleur held back for a minute but in the end they, too, acquiesced. Poor Margie, loyal friend that she was, had to deliver the devastating news to me, along with the reasons. I was quite distraught at first, but then I heard that fib about the lime sherbet punch and the solution to my problem hit me like a ton of bricks! Why couldn't I be the official punch server and cookie hander-outer! You didn't need a date for that!

Margie took my idea back to the committee and it was good news for me! Everyone agreed to let me attend the dance if I'd stay behind the punch bowl all evening, except to use the restroom. I think Miss Corey expressed it best when she said, "Oh, why not? Nobody else ever wants THAT job!"

Dottie Darlin was the only dissenter in the bunch and when she realized she'd been outvoted, Miss Darlin huffed in a rather unattractive way. Then she rudely proclaimed to the rest of the group, "You'll be sorry! Just you wait and see! Trixie'll find a way to mess that up, I'm sure!"

Humph! Well, forget Dottie and her snarky remarks. I could now get into the hop without being thrown out on my kiester. Speaking of "kiester," I always wondered what that funny word meant, but then I figured it out all by myself. I'm ninety-nine percent positive it means "face." Anyway, I'd have to finalize a few minor details, such as how I was going to get to this shindig. My first thought was that I could ride with Cheery Perkins and Gil Snedley. For two weeks straight I tried desperately to run them down (no, not literally, silly), but every time I came to within an inch of them ---- poof! ---- they'd disappear into thin air. Over and over again I heard the same ol' story: "They were here just a second ago. Then I saw Gil get this terrified look in his eyes, grab Cheery by the hand, and shriek, 'Let's get out of here!' It was the strangest thing."

So I was back to Plan A. I'd recently acquired my drivers license, having taken the PHS drivers ed classes twice. Yes, I said twice! The first time there were some tiny glitches, and the second time ---- well, there were some glitches then, too ---- but Coach Goodman finally declared, "Trixie, there's nothing more I can do with you" and decided to give me a passing grade. How nice that he was willing to admit his shortcomings like that. It takes a big man to concede that he's not as capable as he should be. With my drivers license under my belt (literally), I got down on one knee and begged my parents to let me drive myself to the hop. "Please, please, please, may I drive the Sherman tank to the hop? I promise I won't go more than five miles an hour if the roads are snowy!" To my delight, they reluctantly said okay.

The evening of the hop rolled around but it had snowed that afternoon, which meant I couldn't drive more than five miles an hour, which meant I was two hours late getting to the dance. When I finally walked through the doors, holding my bouquet of yellow daisies and wearing my emerald green dress that matched my eyes, I was amazed at the gym's transformation. With beautiful red and green crepe paper streamers dangling from the ceiling and the tables covered in white butcher paper, it no longer looked like our smelly ol' gym. And the wingding was going full blast! Couples were dancing with abandon, laughing like loons and helping themselves to the cookies and punch. Boy howdy, were they helping themselves to the punch! Rushing over to begin my serving duty, I realized it was none too soon. The punch bowl was already three-fourths empty and some of the kids were fiercely elbowing each other to get to what was left.

Not happy with that discourteous behavior, I yelled, "Now listen up!" I'll proudly admit I believe I sounded very much like Coach Goodman. "Get in line and quit acting like goons! If you don't settle down, I'll dump what's left of this punch down the cafeteria sink!"

With that ominous threat hanging over their heads they calmed down a bit, but the girls were still giggling uncontrollably and the guys were even louder than usual, finding every stupid, little thing they said or did hilariously funny. I knew something was definitely out of whack when the 6'5" Barney Flume bent over, camera swaying back and forth from his scrawny neck, winked at me and slurred, "Trixie, yer sooo cute. I never noticed before, but you have the purdiest green eyes. You wanna dance with ----"

"No, thank you very much, Mister Flume. I'm busy doling out the cookies and then I'll need to make some more punch," I primly replied.

"But I don wan a differnt punch, Green Eyes, I like thisss punch. Make more a thisss---- yer sooo cute ----"

"Get outta my sight, Barney Flume! I have work to do!"

Looking a smidge stricken, Barney clutched his cup of punch and staggered away. Then I overheard him slur to

Bonita, "Yer sooo boootiful, Bonita . . . a boootiful name for a boootiful girl ----"

To my great surprise, Bonita seemed to be enjoying Barney's clumsy advances. "Oh, Barney Poo, you have sush a clever way with words . . . you wanna dance with me?"

Boy, all I could make of that nauseating display was that Barney was filled with an extra dose of Christmas spirit and, with it being the holidays, Bonita was filled with extra kindness for a doofus.

After half an hour of pouring cups of punch right and left, as fast as my hands would let me, I began to feel a tad parched myself. I surmised that I, too, could go for a cup since it was obviously very good, considering the way the kids were guzzling it down. But after I took my first sip and before I had a chance to swallow, I immediately spit it out spraying punch all over the Christmas cookies and cutlery and drenching the lollygaggers who refused to leave the punch bowl area. Rather than get mad at my watery explosion, they began licking their sprayed hands and sucking on their wet lapels. Ignoring the bizarreness around me and not wanting to waste one more second, I ran over to the corner table where the chaperones were huddled. Hardly able to speak, I finally blurted out, "The punch has been poisoned! The punch has been poisoned! Quick! Come taste it!" I noticed they were all drinking coffee.

"Oh, good grief, Trixie," drawled Mr. Peabody. "What are

you doing over here? Weren't you supposed to stay behind the punch bowl, unless you had to use the restroom?"

"I know, Mr. Peabody, but there's an emergency! The punch tastes horrible and the only explanation I can come up with is that it's been poisoned. Some lousy, contemptible delinquent dumped kerosene in it! Please hurry! Time is of the essence! The kids are still drinking it!"

Considering the urgency of the situation, I found all the eye-rolling to be quite inappropriate, especially since I was on the verge of tears. At last, nudged on by the others, Pop McNultie pushed himself up from the table and muttered, "Okay, Trixie, let's check out this poisoned punch of yours."

Finally! I took Pop's hand and hurriedly led him back to the refreshment table before any more kids could poison themselves. Brushing Hubert and Ralphie aside, Pop scooped up a ladleful, smelled it, then took a tiny sip. Swallowing that, he took a bigger sip. Downing that, he proceeded to gulp down the whole ladleful!

"Stop it, Pop McNultie! What are you doing? You're going to poison yourself!"

Much too nonchalantly for my liking, Pop replied, "I'll just carry this bowl of punch to the faculty lounge for safe-keeping." And with that, he gingerly carried the bowl away, then quietly told the other chaperones to meet him in the faculty lounge as soon as they could "get rid of" the students.

When Barney noticed what was happening to the

punch, he began pulling on the sleeve of my dress and demanding in a weird voice, "Trissie, whass Misser . . . uh . . . Pops McNultie . . . doing wiss da punch? I wan more ----"

"Oh, shut your pie hole, Barney! Can't you see I'm busy here?" Honestly, that shutterbug could get on my last nerve!

Well, the teachers didn't have to wait long for the gym to clear out, because as soon as the kids realized the punch was gone, they were ready to be gone, too. The chaperones, however, weren't about to let the poisoned students drive.

Coach Goodman pulled me aside and said, "Well, Trixie, since you seem to think you're the best driver in Purdy High, do you suppose you could drive all the kids home, since everyone's been poisoned except for you? The other teachers and I have some important business to tend to in the faculty lounge."

Could I?! Hot diggity dog! If I only drove five miles an hour my parents wouldn't care, I was sure. With all the confidence of a professional race car driver, I replied, "Of course I can! Didn't you hear about how I drove the school bus back from Furnace City after the speech tournament? It will take me a million trips, but I will do it! Even if it takes me the rest of my life!"

The first thing I did was separate the girls from the boys, because everyone knows it's women and children first in times of crisis. After several hours, I managed to get all the giggly girls delivered safely to their abodes, but not without a few complications along the way. It seems Cheery was still smarting from Dottie's brief dalliance with Gil at the previous year's hop and was not happy about it one teensy-weensy bit. I'm not exactly sure how all those old, hostile feelings resurfaced again, but it MIGHT have been when I accidentally said to Cheery, "Wasn't it awful the way Dottie and Gil went to the dance together last year?" So, right there, in the backseat of my '49 Chevy, Cheery confronted Dottie about it again. I guess I shouldn't have put them both back there, but how was I to know a simple date from the year before could almost turn into bloodshed? And then there was Bonita Ruiz who was sobbing uncontrollably because Clarence Waddle was threatening to break up with her once and for all, after he witnessed her flirting unabashedly with that goofball, Barney Flume. Frankly, I took no pity on Bonita this time and took Clarence's side for once. I still don't know what got into her to make her behave like such a gooney bird.

As I began carting the boys home, things got even worse. Ralphie Tittsworth accused me of ruining what could have been one of the best night's of his life. The other guys also seemed to think I'd wrecked their evening. Every last one of them, without exception, acted miffed. When I tried to engage them in conversation, all I got in return were curt "uh-hus" or terse "yeahs." I came to the conclusion that boys are . . . how shall I put this . . . nutty as a fruitcake. It made no sense at all that they should be mad at me when I'd clearly saved them from kerosene poisoning. But, then again, maybe I was just being overly sensitive and they weren't angry at all. I believe it's well known around Purdy High that I'm extremely sensitive and completely aware of everything going on around me. Nothing gets past this gal.

By the time I dropped off the last guy, Hubert Button, it was already daylight. Like all the others, he didn't even smile as he got out of the Chevy, let alone offer to help pay for gas or give me a small tip for my perfect driving skills. Oh well, I couldn't be worried about a few crabby kids, not when I knew I'd just saved the lives of every young Purdy Squirrel who'd attended the Christmas Hop. No one would die of kerosene poisoning on my watch! You're welcome, Purdy High!

# JULY 4ᵗʰ JAILBIRD

Purdy's July 4ᵗʰ celebrations in the early Sixties were great times! Besides all the hoopla at the fairgrounds with horse races and rodeos, the downtown area, especially on the Yippee County Courthouse Plaza, was a bustle of activity. There were booths all around the plaza, sponsored by the various civic and school organizations, selling everything from hamburgers to candy apples. The Purdy High School Lettermen's Club was in charge of the "jail" in the summer of 1964 and I volunteered to help. Well, what red-blooded American girl wouldn't? The PHS lettermen were going to be hanging around!

The week surrounding July 4ᵗʰ was called "Dress Western Week" which meant that people were expected to dress in western wear when venturing into downtown Purdy, and specifically if meandering around the Plaza. The jail was a makeshift cage where people who weren't in cowboy clothes were stuck and not let out until they paid a fine, which was then donated to a charity. City slickers, like the people from Furnace City, were easy targets, but the tiniest infraction warranted a visit to the calaboose. I always thought this was loads of fun and more than fair, until I was the one tossed in the hoosegow.

What was my drastic offense? Penny loafers! Unlike many of my classmates who were real cowgirls, living and working on the surrounding family ranches, I wasn't a real cowgirl. The only animal I ever tended was my German Shepherd, Queenie. I couldn't afford a pair of cowboy boots on my dollar-an-hour salary from La Belle Beauty Shop and my parents certainly couldn't be expected to shell out their hard-earned dough for such expensive footwear that was worn only once a year, so there I was, stuck with penny loafers. I didn't mind, until Clarence Waddle eyed my tootsies.

"Okay, Trixie, in you go! You may have on jeans and a cowgirl shirt, but those shoes are definitely not western!" remarked Clarence, the current president of the PHS Lettermen's Club.

"But, Clarence, can't you loan me some money for bail?" I begged.

"No way, Trixie. Besides, I seem to remember losing my cowboy hat at the Yippee County Fair, after you gave us all that free ride on the Ferris wheel. I never did find my hat. I don't have enough money to buy a new one, much less bail you out of jail. And now you want me to let you go? Ha! Fat chance! Get in there!"

As I began protesting, "But Clarence ----" he cut in.

"And another thing, you little kook. You were the one who got our delicious punch taken away at the Christmas Hop! I'll never forgive you for that!" As Clarence came behind and encircled my waist with his hairy arms, which reminded me of Queenie's tail, he began dragging me into the jail. Off to the side I spotted a grinning Dickie Darlin, one of Purdy High's track stars, observing the whole scene. Since he was Dottie's brother, and Dottie was an okay friend, I thought maybe I could enlist his aid. "Dickie, help me! These penny loafers aren't a big deal and ----"

"You're right, kiddo," interjected the tall, dark and handsome Dickie. "The penny loafers aren't a big deal, but nearly running me down in that drivers ed car, and causing me to race across McNultie Field to get away from you . . . IS! Now get in there!" he yelled, in a very unlettermanly way.

"My incarceration is of no benefit to the wonderful people of Purdy. I'm not a dangerous criminal!" I wailed to anyone who would listen.

"Criminal, no. Dangerous, yes!" hollered most of the guys in unison.

Humph! Since Dickie was obviously not going to be of assistance, I looked around and spotted another friend . . . well . . . possible friend. "Hubert Button! Hey, remember how we cut up that cat or skunk or whatever it was in biology together? You never would have passed that class without me! How 'bout a little help over here?"

Hubert frowned at me. "Passed the class, yes. With a

lousy 'C.' Without your crummy help I would have gotten an 'A.' So thanks for nothing. And you never did bake me those brownies you promised. And I haven't forgotten how you poked me with the whitewash stick because you thought I was lollygagging on "P" Mountain? Honestly, Trixie, sometimes I wonder why you haven't been put in jail long before this! Now, be a good girl and take your medicine. Or pay the twenty-cent fine. Your choice."

"Bbbutt . . . these penny loafers were bought at WESTERN Auto! Doesn't that count for something? And I baked you those brownies; it's just that they never made it past first period. And I don't have any more money! I spent my last dime on that box of popcorn, which, by the way . . . get your grubby mitts out of it, Dickie! It's my lunch!"

"Here, take your precious popcorn and go sit down over there in that corner. Maybe one of your girl friends will loan you twenty cents," Dickie said, handing me the popcorn while shoving me into the clink and turning to talk to Kitty Shrub who'd just sidled up alongside him.

"Kitty! Kitty! Am I still spending the night at your house? I already told my mom, so she's not expecting me home tonight. And, while I think of it, can you loan me twenty cents to get out of here?" I said, interrupting her chat with Dickie, who she had a huge crush on, as did every other girl in PHS. Except for me now. I thought he was a brat.

"Sorry, but my cousins from Furnace City are up for the weekend, so you can't come over tonight," Kitty explained, "but Mom says you can come next week, if you want. She really likes you because she says you're so sweet and mannerly. But so far as loaning you any money, I don't think so. You still haven't paid me back that quarter for the Dracula movie, or the dime for the Purdy Stage, or the six cents for the two milks I bought you in the cafeteria, or the twenty cents for the popcorn and candy I paid for at the Moose Theater, or the ----"

"Yeah, yeah, I get the picture, Kitty. Never mind. You just run along and have fun and don't give a second thought to poor me sitting all alone rotting away in this stinkin' jail cell and ----"

"Okay, I won't. See ya later alligator!"

Being mad as a wet hen, I absolutely refused to say "after while crocodile" back to her. I was hoping that would make her feel bad. Then I watched her stroll away, hand in hand, with (stupid) Dickie. So much for my revenge.

I went back to munching on my popcorn when Lulu Dilly walked by, clutching a hot dog in one hand, cotton candy in the other. I never could figure out where that tiny thing put all that food. "Lulu! Over here!" Lulu abruptly turned her head, saw me standing behind the bars and began laughing hysterically. Ignoring her temporary insanity, I continued, "Can you loan me twenty cents to get out of here?"

"Oh . . . golly . . . Trixie . . . I'd like to," she stammered, trying to stifle her rude chuckles, "but I just spent my last penny and rules are rules." Then she smugly added, in between laughs, "You, of all people, should know that. You're the one always spouting your mouth off about the rules!"

I self-righteously snorted a couple of times. I glared at her and answered in the snottiest voice I could muster. "Really, Lulu? You're the one who talked me into ditching girls chorus and now you're preaching to me about rules?" As she sauntered away, pulling at her cotton candy and shoving it in her mouth as fast as she could, I thought about how she'd knocked me for a loop with all that blabbering about rules. Lulu, of all people!

About this time, Barney Flume walked by, sporting his customary camera-necklace. Catching sight of me in my new surroundings, he carefully approached, then began fiddling with the flashbulbs. Before he could say, "Cheese," I screeched, "Don't you dare take a picture of me in this joint, Barney Flume! If you so much as raise that camera of yours or even LOOK like you're going to take my picture, I will strangle you with my bare paws!" I made a wringing motion with my hands to show I meant business.

"Gee whiz, Trixie, you're so cute when you're mad," replied the knucklehead Barney.

"Well, if you think I'm so darn cute, how about loaning me some money to get out of here?"

"Uh . . . you're not THAT cute," said the so-called photographer. Then FLASH! and off he trotted to capture on film some other unsuspecting victim.

Man, oh man. I felt as though I'd been blinded! The

next time I laid eyes on that Barney Flume I was going to ---- ! But if I couldn't get that nincompoop to loan me some money, I was doomed. Maybe I should try begging from people who didn't know me. Maybe that was my problem; people knew me, and my history, too well. I decided to aim for the obvious non-Purdyonians instead. They were easy to recognize, the people wearing really new, fashionable clothes and several pieces of jewelry, not just a Timex watch. When they'd walk by I'd call out in my most courteous voice, "Excuse me, but could you please loan me some money?" In response I'd usually get, "Oh, look, Henry, they've got an actress in there pretending to beg for money. What Purdy won't do to make their July 4th celebrations the best in the state!" I even offered to sell kisses through the bars for a nickel, but there were no takers.

I gave up! I resigned myself to spending time in the slammer and sat down on one of the bales of hay in the corner. It was a little hard to see the parade from my vantage point, but I could make out the Purdy Parade Queen. She was none other than my second best friend, Bonita Ruiz. Not only was Bonita as cute as a button, but she could ride a horse as expertly as Dale Evans. And if that weren't enough to make her the best queen Purdy had ever seen, her dad was Queenie's vet. I was so proud of her and called her name when she rode by. "Hey, Bonita! Over here! In the jail!" Evidently she couldn't hear me, but several of the horses could. They got spooked and began rearing up. Worried that I may have started something, I retreated to my bale of hay, much to the relief of everyone, including all the lettermen.

From my seat on the hay, if I craned my neck really hard, I could view parts of the floats that were sponsored by the dude ranches, summer camps, civic organizations and PHS clubs. Of course the school band I didn't need to witness, as its racket could be heard for a mile. The shiny horses, all decked out in fancy gear, many showing off braided manes and tails, were difficult to see. The riders were a little easier to make out and I recognized most of them as being classmates at Purdy High.

When the parade was over and things around the Plaza began to quiet down a tad, I found myself slipping off one of the hay bales and falling in between it and the one behind. After the difficult morning I'd endured, a nice siesta sounded good, so I decided to take advantage of the comfortable hay bed. I'd heard a couple of girls at school talking about a roll in the hay, and it sounded fun, so I thought I'd give it a try. I rolled around in the hay to get good and comfy and the next thing you know I was sound asleep in between the two bales.

It seems that during the course of the late afternoon and evening no one realized I was still in the jail. Every letterman assumed another had let me out and no one bothered to check. Hubert thought Purdy Police Chief, Kurt Langley, might have opened the door, stating, "You know what a soft heart he has. He's always picking up stray

animals and can never resist Trixie's emerald green eyes."
Ralphie thought it was probably Coach Goodman who'd
done the deed: "Trixie's his favorite babysitter, you know.
Everyone at school knows she's his pet. You can never say
a bad word against her with him around." Davey had to
admit that Mr. Richley might have let me out, since he
knew the speech teacher trusted me completely, having
chosen me to drive the speech team back to Purdy from
Furnace City one time. So, nobody knew exactly what had
happened to me. They just "knew" I was no longer in the
cell.

I've always been a sound sleeper, so I didn't wake up
when, from time to time, other delinquents were thrown
in the jail with me. And, being the genteel gal that I am, I
am not prone to the dreadful habit of snoring; therefore,
I did not alert anyone to my presence by emitting ugly,
unladylike honking or braying noises. When all the booths
and jail were shut down at ten o'clock that night, I was out
like a light. I never once heard the cowboys parading in
and out of the famous Purdy Bar or noisily staggering up
and down Bourbon Row.

Around seven o'clock the next morning, something
woke me up. Yawning and stretching and trying to gather
my bearings, I started to remember what had happened.
I glanced at my Timex ---- still ticking ---- and began
picking bits of straw out of my hair and teeth. Then I went
for the door and realized my predicament. Just as I was all
set to start screaming my lungs out, my best friend, Margie

Sweetum, came scurrying by carrying an ice cream maker. What luck! Good ol' Margie!

"Psst! Margie! Over here!"

"Trixie! What on earth are you doing? Stop goofing around and get outta there!"

"What am I doing? Baking a pie! What's it look like?"

"Well, you don't have to get snippy about it. Were you in there all night?"

"Um . . . I guess so. I'm wearing the same clothes and I don't remember anything since yesterday, so ---- Look, Margie, I need a bobby pin to pick this lock. Take that one out of your hair bow and pick this lock! I'm starving!" I began scouring the ground for a few fallen popcorn kernels. "Oh, good. There's one."

"Trixie, why don't I run over to the pay phone and call Police Chief Langley. He'll know how to get you out," offered Margie, trying to be helpful.

"No, Margie, no! I don't want the whole town to know I'm in here! I haven't brushed my teeth or anything. I'm certainly not ready to be on the front page of The Purdy Evening Courier looking like this. No, just try picking the lock with that bobby pin. Don't worry, your hair looks fine without the red bow."

While I was trying to find something else I could eat off the jail cell floor, dainty Margie began fiddling around with the hair pin and lock. She fiddled and fiddled until I thought I'd strangle myself ----or Margie! I finally grabbed the bobby pin out of her hand and, in sheer frustration, squawked, "Gimme that! Here, I'll show you how to pick a lock!" I bent the pin, stuck it in the lock, jiggled it around a bit and voila! The door pushed open!

"Wow, Trixie! That's quite a feat. Where'd you ever learn to do that?"

"Just you never mind, Margie. It's best you don't know." Then, expertly changing the subject, I inquired, "Where are you going with that ice cream maker? I guess you're going to be making some ice cream, huh? What kind are you going to make? Is it for the drama club? How much are you selling it for? What's the club going to do with all the money you make? Is it easy to ma ---- ?"

"Oh, give it up, Trixie. I don't give a hoot about where you learned to pick locks! I've gotta go. The drama club is waiting for the ice cream maker. Go home and brush your hair. You look like a plowed-over scarecrow! Toodle-oo!"

Thinking I'd better start walking home, I happened to glance down and right there, smack dab where my right foot was going to land, was a shiny dime! Just enough to get me on the Purdy Stage and back to my house! Boy, this was turning out to be my lucky day! I figured I was overdue for some good luck, considering the harrowing night I'd endured. Well, I couldn't actually remember anything about the night, but it MUST have been harrowing. Then I stopped dead in my tracks and looked down at my feet! My penny loafers! Each holding a brand new dime! Two dimes! Twenty cents! I'd had the bail money all along!

Looking back on my ordeal, I came to the conclusion

that, despite everything, at least I still had my twenty cents. And let the record show that my superb lock-picking skills were never used for evil ---- except for that one desperate time in Albuquerque.

# HAY RIDE GONE WILD

During the early Sixties, there was a really neat farm outside of Purdy that was owned by the Young family. I don't mean they WERE young; in fact, the parents had to have been at least forty! I mean their last name was Young. Just like I was a Poor. It didn't necessarily mean I WAS poor, despite our '49 Chevy. It just meant that Grandpa had decided to drop the "e" at the end. Anywho, Mr. and Mrs. Young had several kids, one of whom was in my class at good ol' PHS and had the name of Buckley, or Buck as I affectionately called him. The Youngs and I attended the same Methodist Church on Curley Street, a street that would be called Main Street in any other town. I guess the Youngs liked to help the kids in Purdy, because for Halloween in 1964, members of the Methodist Youth Fellowship and their guests were invited to the farm for a hay ride. I was President of MYF for the second year in a row. This fact has nothing much to do with the story; I just like to brag about being president.

Young's Farm was everything you'd expect a good old-fashioned family farm to be. All kinds of vegetables were grown, including the famous pumpkins for Halloween. At Thanksgiving their turkeys were considered the best by everybody, from residents of Podunk, one hundred miles to the north, to the big metropolis of Furnace City, one hundred miles to the south. Of course everything was organic, although we didn't use that word. We said fresh.

At long last the day of the hay ride arrived and my fellow MYFers and I, along with our guests, met at the church. My parents had very generously allowed me to drive our '49 Chevy, aka The Sherman Tank, provided I took only six passengers. Of course everyone wanted to ride with me, since I was by far the best driver in PHS ---- just ask Coach Goodman, or me, if you don't believe me! By the way, there's a man who DID live up to his name, Goodman! To avoid any unnecessary bloodshed caused by people fighting over who was going to ride with me, I put everyone's name in Gil Snedley's cowboy hat, then meticulously picked out six lucky riders. As we then piled into our assigned cars, all I heard from my riders was, "I'm so glad I get to ride with you, Trixie," and "You're such a great driver," and "I feel so safe with you behind the wheel," ---- you know, little truisms like that. There was only one groan and that came from Cheery Perkins, who wanted to ride with Gil. Her reason? "Gil's cuter." WELL! First of all, I don't know what Gil had that I didn't, since the really sharp kids in the school seemed to find me quite adorable; and second of all, not ONE word was mentioned about what a much better driver I was than her boyfriend! Cheery seemed to place no importance on that whatsoever! Honestly, she was always stuck with Gil; you'd think she'd want a break once in a while.

Fortunately, the half-hour drive ended up being quite pleasant, despite Cheery's constant whining about not being with you-know-who. When we finally arrived at the farm, Mrs. Young and her daughter, Sally, had prepared homemade apple cider for us. Mr. Young and Buck were hitching up a horse to the wagon, which was stacked with bales of hay for benches (the wagon, not the horse). Quickly finishing our drinks, we jumped on the wagon to claim a seat. Buck was going to be our driver and since I had a whopper of a crush on him, I yelled "Shotgun!" Not hesitating a second, however, he rather rudely informed me that no one was going to sit up front with him: "Get in the back with everybody else, Trixie."

Buck didn't seem to understand my status, so I tried explaining: "Bbuut . . . er . . . Buck . . . I"M THE PRESIDENT OF MYF!"

To that he insisted, "I don't care if you're the President of the USSR. Get in the back!"

Giving up I relented, "Humph! Whatever you say . . . BuckLEY ----!"

So off we went, trotting along the narrow dirt paths that skirted the corn fields. Some of the kids began singing and a couple of delinquents started smooching ---- you know who you are, Cheery and Gil! Well, I was going to have none of that! To take their minds off such shenanigans, I began telling jokes. Everyone in school loved my jokes, most of which I got out of Cracker Jack boxes or Bazooka bubble gum wrappers. Naturally the kids were enthralled, but unfortunately for them I soon ran out of jokes. In order to keep them entertained, I began recounting a story: "I was hiding behind some bushes after a football game, and you'll never guess what I saw! And you'll never guess who was doing that!" Everyone started snickering nervously, including Cheery, whose laugh could be heard all the way to Purdy, when all of a sudden the horse began rearing up.

As Buck was trying to calm the skittish equine, a huge menacing-looking bumble bee appeared, stinging the poor nag on the rump (the horse, not Cheery). Utterly spooked, the horse then bolted like a bat outta hell and off we charged, bouncing across the corn fields as fast as the horse's legs could carry him. This started everyone screaming at the top of their lungs! Buck was frantically attempting to gain control, but as the reins flew out of his hands and he was tossed like Raggedy Andy out of the wagon, the nag raced on, leaving poor Buck far behind, gasping in a cloud of dust.

There we were, helpless as a Purdy kid in downtown Timbuktu, clutching each other in the back of a runaway hay wagon, while the choking driver slowly receded into the background! As everyone looked behind for help, I, as always, looked forward! I realized what I had to do! I leaped from my bale of hay and scrambled to the driver's bench. At that precise moment, a particularly deadly ear of corn ---- in fact, the largest ear of corn ever recorded in our state ---- smacked me upside the head, causing a small, but significantly visible, dent! Ignoring that, as well as the wooden splinters from the bench that were impaling my backside, I struggled to gather the reins, while hollering repeatedly, "Whoa, Trigger! Whoa, Trigger!" Nothing happened. Maybe his name wasn't Trigger. "Whoa, Silver!" Still no cooperation."Whoa, Mister Ed!" Nothing.

From behind me, I could hear the kids shrieking, "Do something, Trixie! Help us! We're scared!"

Well, that did it! No innocent Squirrel on my watch was going to be scared! "Listen up, you four-legged overgrown dog! You stop right now, whatever-your-name-is, or when I get my hands around your scrawny neck you'll wish you'd -----"

That did the trick! The horse abruptly stopped! That, in itself, was a good thing, however several untethered kids were flung into the pumpkin patch, causing mushy orange-colored innards to be splattered from one end of the farm to the other! The kids who weren't flown into midair had splinters of straw embedded in their palms from grabbing the bales for dear life! Cheery and Gil, who were clinging onto the bales and each other, were wearing matching wool sweaters. At first glance, they looked like a giant pin cushion. All in all, it wasn't a pretty sight, but no one was complaining; they were all simply grateful to me for having saved them.

Once Buck caught up with the wagon and I'd scraped the slimy pumpkin goo off the kids, as well as plucked needles of straw out of their mitts, I ordered Petunia ---- yes, that was her name---- to get a goin'. She obeyed without batting an eyelash. Good thing. I didn't want to have to go through THAT again! Of course, and I shall try my best to be mature and refrain from saying I told you so, we never would have had that runaway problem if Buck had let me ride shotgun as I wanted to in the first place. He really should have listened to me. Oh, I can't do it! I TOLD YOU SO!

So that's the story of a Halloween hay ride gone wild, but tamed in the end by an enormously brave, yet oh-so-humble, Purdy Squirrel girl. Once again, there was a happy ending thanks to me! You're welcome, Purdy High!

# LIGHTING
# THE CHRISTMAS SEASON

The Lighting of the Yippee County Courthouse was one of the most exciting traditions of the '64 Christmas season in Purdy. It was quite a celebration unto itself, with townsfolk flooding the Plaza to join in. On the first Saturday in December ---- but not before! ---- we Purdyonians would gather together to officially begin the Christmas season and to rejoice in the spectacular annual display of lights.

I was part of the organized festivities as a very important member of the Purdy High School Mixed Chorus. Our director, a proud man of Scottish ancestry, was the very handsome Mr. Campbell, who occasionally would wear his skirt ---- er, I mean, kilt ---- and play his bagpipe in class. I wasn't crazy about that bagpipe, since it evoked terrible memories of the time I was riding my bike and accidentally ran over the tail of Mr. Crabtree's cat. Mr. Campbell was an extremely dedicated and good teacher, even if he had once impulsively yanked the loudspeaker out of the music room wall when the unwanted voice over it had irritated him. Naturally I didn't blame my teacher. The ladies in the administration office should have known full well that Mr. Campbell did not like his classes interrupted, especially right before statewide competitions. But, most of the time, our director was on a relatively even keel, which produced enviable results in the rivalries.

It was on a cold, brisk December evening that we members of the choir stood patiently on the courthouse steps, anticipating Mr. Campbell's first hand signal to sing. We'd been diligently rehearsing the Christmas carols since the middle of October, so we were more than well prepared. Every section of the choir sang beautifully, however it must be noted that the altos were particularly outstanding; as one might deduce, I sang alto.

"We'll sing O Little Town of Bethlehem," Mr. Campbell informed us, "and then the Christmas lights will come on." Always the obedient students, we sang our little hearts out and we sounded great ---- especially the altos ---- but nothing happened with the lights. Not knowing what was going on, we began squirming and whispering among ourselves. Then we noticed the worried faces and heard the murmurs of concern: "What's going on? Why aren't the lights coming on?"

As more and more time passed, I could tell panic was starting to set in, as children began to weep and adults began wringing their hands. Finally, in sheer desperation,

Mayor Floyd Toot approached the microphone and pleaded, "Is there anyone present who can fix the lights?"

Of course I knew who could, but I remained modestly silent, which was no small feat, I can tell you! Then every single member of the chorus, as well as Mr. Campbell, pointed directly at me and shouted in unison, "Trixie can! She can do EVERYTHING!"

Well, my usual humility prevented me from boasting that I could do EVERYTHING, but it was common knowledge around PHS, and all of Purdy, that I could do ALMOST everything (the exception being geometry), so I was pretty sure I could tackle this little problem, too. I will admit that for this particular glitch, I was at an advantage. My dad was an electrician by trade and I'd been watching him plug cords into wall sockets my whole life ---- it was in my blood! Also, I knew not to play my electric radio on the side of the tub when I was taking my bubble bath. And not only that, but in Mr. Reinagle's typing class I'd saved the day plenty of times when the electric typewriters had blown a fuse after some smarty pants like my best friend, Bonita Ruiz, had typed over two hundred words a minute! When such a calamity occurred, I'd rush over to the fuse box and perform my magic. Mr. Reinagle appeared to be eternally grateful, but never grateful enough to give me an A. He always tried to rationalize this injustice by stating, "Trixie, typing three words a minute will NOT get you an A, no matter how many blown fuses you claim to fix."

Back to the disaster . . . I knew time was of the essence.

How could the Christmas season begin without the brilliant, colorful lights to illuminate the courthouse? I urgently grabbed the hand of Lulu Dilly, a tiny pixie of a girl and my favorite alto buddy, and off we dashed to make sure everything was plugged in correctly. (I can't tell you how many times good money was paid to an electrician, only to be told the toaster had come unplugged!) With that simple task checked off, I latched onto Lulu again and we made a beeline for the basement of the courthouse. It was my expert opinion that's where we'd find the fuse box. And was I right? Of course! I opened the box and AHA! NOT to my surprise, there was in fact a blown fuse!

I'm nothing, if not prepared for emergencies, so into my gunny sack of a purse I began digging ---- ChapStick, Kleenex, Iodine and Band-Aids, Juicy Fruit gum --- where, oh where, was that doggone 15 amp fuse? Becoming exasperated, and nearly cutting off my finger with a steak knife lying on the very bottom, I finally found it! As quickly as I could, I replaced the defective fuse, then rushed back to the switch on the side of the courthouse, dragging a panting Lulu along behind. Instructing my loyal, out-of-breath helper to stay put and wait for my signal, I quickly raced up the stairs to join the throng of expectant revelers. With a firm "thumbs up" for Lulu to hit the switch, the magnificent Christmas lights set the Plaza aglow! At that precise moment, the choir burst into "Hallelujah!" as every face turned toward me in thankful adoration.

As the strains of "Hallelujah" infused radiant downtown

Purdy with glorious music, I found myself overwhelmed with the realization that once again I'd saved the day. The churches could have their pageants; the schools could plan their Christmas programs; the families could begin preparations for their holiday traditions. All the Christmas festivities could now proceed without delay ---- thanks to me and my superb electrical skills. You're welcome, Purdy!

# SLIPPERY ROCK DITCH DAY

The main motivation I had for graduating from good ol' PHS was senior ditch day! Most of the classes over the years had gone to Slippery Rock, that wonderful area a little south of Podunk that combined smooth, red rocks with cool, running water. This was okay if you wanted to be like everybody else, but I was always a little different, or so people said, and I had a much better idea! Paris, France! We seniors could combine our resources and have bake sales, car washes, and ice cream socials in order to raise enough money for us all to go. I was an expert at those activities, having done a million of them during my high school years. I could easily spearhead all the committees.

If the major deterrent to going to Paris was the language, well, I had that problem covered too. I could be the translator. I was quite fluent in French, having taken two years with Mrs. Snotgrass. It must be noted, however, that I had spent a good deal of class time in Mr. Rizzo's office for talking while Snotty was trying to, but I nevertheless felt confident in my fluency. I wasn't quite sure how French was supposed to sound because we never spoke it in class, but I had finished translating The Count of Monte Cristo from the back of the book before anyone else. On Tuesdays and Fridays I ate only french fries for lunch and on Sundays my mom always made french toast. Not only that, but I'd gotten a "B" on my notebook of France; that's almost an "A" to my way of thinking. In my beautiful, slaved-over notebook, I'd pasted pictures of France that I'd cut out of old National Geographic magazines and I'd written at length about the number of bottles of Champagne consumed every year, not only in France, but in the whole wide world! Not to brag, but my notebook really was an excellent achievement and definitely should have received the top grade. And not just in my class, but in all the French classes! But, as was common knowledge throughout Purdy High, Snotty had a grudge against me. I'm not sure how everyone heard about this, other than my telling anyone who would listen, but facts are facts. And last, but certainly not least, there was Brigitte. Brigitte was my real-life French pen pal who lived on the outskirts of gay Paree. We wrote to each other once or twice a year! It was usually in English, but I think it should still count toward my resume for translator.

I presented my fantastique idea about going to la belle France to the stupid council . . . er, I mean . . . the student council and what kind of a response did I get?

"That's the goofiest thing I've ever heard in my life,

Trixie! You've come up with some loo-loos, but this one takes the cake! Do you lie awake at night thinking up these cornball ideas? You're a swell enough kid and all, but sometimes I think -----"

"Okay, okay," I interrupted. "I get the point, Mr. Bunson." So that was that. Those narrow-minded squares outvoted me; the seniors were headed for Slippery Rock ---- AGAIN.

Our trip was on a Friday in late May and the weather was perfect; no, I'm not going to try and take credit for that. After we loaded onto the bus I immediately made everybody sing that popular little ditty, "Ninety-nine Bottles of Beer on the Wall." They all joined in, with varying degrees of reluctance, except for a couple of delinquents in the back who were trying to neck without Mr. Peabody and Mr. Nikniewicz seeing them. You know who you are - Lulu Dilly and Hubert Button!

Ralphie Tittsworth couldn't grasp the notion of counting backward, so he quietly mumbled the numbers. After thirteen verses, when the rest of us were at eighty-six, Ralphie bellowed, "A hunnert an twelve!"

Holy cow! Everyone rolled their eyes, well aware of Ralphie's quirk ---- we'd been on road trips with him before ---- and we started over. From then on, whenever he opened his mouth, we threw Fritos at him hoping to hit the huge, gaping target. Ralphie enjoyed the game, and the Fritos.

We finally arrived at Slippery Rock at bottle number eighteen. We were thrilled to get off the bus and start enjoying the slick rocks, kept that way by the stream cascading over them. It was an idyllic natural slide, not meant for tomfoolery. Clowning around, however, seemed to come naturally to certain guys and these guys had to start showing off for the girls. Even though the ladies weren't paying one teensy-weensy bit of attention to them, Hubert Button, Davey Goodnuff and Ralphie decided it would be a good idea to slide down the rocks, headfirst, on their stomachs. Clarence Waddle and Stanley Weiss held back for a sec then they, too, joined their knucklehead friends.

Over and over again, down they slid, hollering idiotic gibberish like "Geronimo!" After about half an hour, realizing that no girls would be swarming all over them, these bozos finally dragged themselves out of the water and began examining their pathetic bags of bones. What a hideous, battered sight they all were! Their bellies, knees and noses looked like someone had smeared them with ketchup.

While the heartless Lulu, Margie, Bonita and Kitty started pointing at them and laughing hysterically, I, always the mature one, reached into my pink, plastic beach bag and pulled out a bottle of Iodine and some self-stick bandages, all securely wrapped in waxed paper.

"Come here you guys! This'll fix you up good as new!" I yelled.

Spotting the Iodine before the others, Hubert shrieked, "Oh my gosh! She's got Iodine! Run for your lives!" Ralphie glanced at the potent little bottle and began heading for the aspen trees.

Davey began screaming like a little four-year-old girl, "Get that stuff away from us, you ghoul!"

"Ghoul?" I shouted back. "Florence Nightingale or Clara Barton's more like it! Now get over here and let me douse your wounds!"

Obviously terrified of medical professionals, Hubert and Davey tried to get away from me by holding their breath and plunging back into the water. Clarence disappeared into thin air and was not seen again until we got on the bus to go to the roller rink, at which time he crawled out from under one of the seats.

The only scaredy cat I did manage to tackle was Stanley. It wasn't easy, because he was one of the stars of the PHS track team, but when he slipped and fell flat on his face, I plopped myself down on his ankles and tried to get the Iodine open. Then he made me an offer I couldn't refuse: "Please, Trixie, let me go! If you do, I'll do your geometry homework 'til the end of school!"

Stanley knew my Achilles' heel, all right! I quit fiddling with the Iodine and declared, "Deal!"

With Stanley out of my clutches, I ran back to the water and waited for Hubert and Davey to resurface. After a couple of minutes they finally came up, sputtering and spitting water straight into my face. Then, terror in their eyes as they spied my Iodine, they sucked in a huge gulp of air and went under again.

Oh, good grief! I didn't have all day! I left the submerged Hubert and Davey to fend for themselves and scurried over to Ralphie, whose turquoise and red swimming trunks could be seen a mile away behind that skinny aspen.

"Ralphie, get out here right now and let me put some of this medicine on you! If you don't, you're liable to get scurvy or some such nasty disease!"

"Please, Trixie, please, I'll do your geometry homework," Ralphie begged.

"I've already got that covered. What else you got?"

"How 'bout I wash and wax your Sherman tank every week?"

"Deal!" Considering the size of that '49 Chevy, he'd be looking at hours of rubbing and buffing.

Well, I hadn't succeeded in rendering aid to any of the goons, which deflated me, I must admit, especially since I was a prominent Red Cross candy striper. Feeling a tad defeated, I quietly went to stand behind some trees and watch all those fraidy cats scamper behind Pop McNultie, who seemed to be laughing his head off about something. Sounding like the Tower of Babel, those chickens began tattling on me and my Iodine. I eavesdropped as hard as I could, but all I could make out were bits and pieces:

". . . nutty as a fruitcake . . ."

". . . should be expelled . . ."

". . . crazy as a loon . . ."

At that moment the only thing I could think of was how ignorant they all were about medicine. I guess they'd never been taught that, unless a medicine is excruciatingly painful, it isn't killing the germs properly. Oh well . . . let them all die of the black plague! See if I cared!

Lunchtime soon rolled around and, let me tell you, I was pretty worn out from chasing those hooligans all over Slippery Rock! But I knew that once I finished my Skippy peanut butter sandwich (a whole one today), bag of Fritos and Snickers candy bar, I'd be off and running again! And when I got wind of where we were headed next, I really perked up! We were going to a real, honest-to-goodness roller skating rink!

We all hopped on the bus again, the same bus Clarence Waddle was hiding in, and took off down the winding, two-lane road. I couldn't believe we were going to an actual roller rink, since my usual one was a run-down tennis court next to the Purdy Park. Bonita Ruiz and I would go there so I could teach her all my nifty tennis and roller skating moves. It wasn't a great place, full of zillions of cracks and potholes, but it was somewhat better than the roads.

Unfortunately, on this very important day, I didn't have my own skates ---- the neat kind you clip onto your shoes. I'd somehow lost the special skate key I always wore on a purple string around my neck. I wasn't sure where I'd lost it, but it might have been when I took it off to wash the '49 Chevy. I think a chipmunk probably saw it on the ground, picked it up with his pointy, little, yellow teeth, and hid it in a tree hole. I've thought and thought about it and that's the only thing that makes any sense.

Well, phooey! Without my own skates, I'd be stuck wearing the crummy shoe-skates the rink doled out. When I went to the counter and told my size to the oddball standing behind said counter, I was greeted with some alarming news! All they had left was a man's size eleven and a lady's size four. Since my tootsies took a perfect size seven, I found myself in a definite quandary (fancy talk for pickle). Having no other choice, I first tried on the elevens, but my feet were wobbling like a stick of Juicy Fruit that had been sitting on the Chevy's dashboard all afternoon. After sixteen head-on collisions with extremely careless fellow skaters and one very close call with a hostile pinball machine, I decided to switch to the fours.

Since it was common knowledge that I was the best skater in the PHS senior class, Mr. Peter Pitman, my civics teacher, insisted I skate with him. There were a lot of cute boys I would have preferred to skate with, but since my grade in Mr. Pitman's class could use all the help it could get, I figured I'd better oblige. Again, I won't mention those guys' names, lest their current wives become insanely jealous and come after me! So round and round the rink Mr. Pitman and I skated, in the same ol' boring oval, as I kept thinking, "Your grade's improving, Trixie. Your grade's improving."

I thought I was an outstanding skater until I caught a glimpse of someone who was spectacular! I was positive this amazing athlete was the Olympic gold medal winner, Miss Peggy Fleming! I'd heard she was a fairly decent ice skater, but it appeared she was a darn good roller skater as well. She was performing double toe loops, back to back triple Axels and breathtaking forward twizzles ---- all to Chuck Berry's Twist song! Holy Cow! It was mind-boggling! But then, on closer inspection, I realized it wasn't Miss Fleming at all but my very own P.E. teacher, Miss Corey. I hadn't noticed the blue hair at first.

Well, since I looked up to Miss Corey so much, I told Mr. Pitman we needed to rev things up a bit and follow her neat example. We'd start with a simple flip jump, after which he'd catch me and fling me over his head with one arm, while I twirled around in a few flying spins; then we'd execute a couple of backward swizzles, add in some crossovers and quadruple Axels, just for good measure, and finally finish with the ever-popular Death Spiral!

Mr. Pitman listened intently to my instructions as his sensitive brown eyes slowly began to cross. Then he reached into his back pocket and whipped out a tattered, greasy, brown paper bag, which was obviously left over from his sack lunch that day. Slowly and rhythmically he began breathing into it: in . . . out . . . in . . . out. He was as white as Miss Corey's hair when she'd forget to put the midnight blue rinse on it. After Mr. Pitman was finally able to take in air like a normal person, without the help of that dopey bag that smelled faintly of tuna fish, he staggered over to the folding chairs, grabbed onto one for dear life, and collapsed semi-conscious, arms dangling to the floor. Oh, good grief! The way he was carrying on, you'd have thought I'd asked him to do something really crazy like climb Mt. Everest all by himself or give me an A+ in civics, instead of kicking around a few simple skate moves!

Well, that put an end to my skating, but to be perfectly frank, that suited me just fine. My dogs were killing me and I had this terrible fear that I'd done irreparable damage to them, thanks to those crummy skates. I asked my good buddy, Margery Sweetum, if she'd go into the restroom with me to check them out. I was afraid to face the horror alone.

"Oh, all right, Trixie, but let's hurry up about it. Billy Bunson just asked me to skate with him and you know I've had a crush on him since seventh grade."

Margie followed me into the restroom, where I sat on the floor to remove my skates and socks. Steeling myself for the inevitable, I at last dared to look at my feet and sure enough! Just as I feared! "Look, Margery, a water blister! I told you I had serious problems!"

"You have serious problems, all right, but they have nothing to do with your feet, Trixie," drawled Margie, showing no compassion whatsoever. "It's no big deal. Stop being such a nut."

Shocked by her callousness, I informed her that I wanted a second opinion. "Get Kitty Shrub in here. Her mom's a nurse, so she should know a little something about my dire situation ---- certainly a lot more than YOU, Miss Margie!"

Margie's reply was a haughty sniff, but she did depart to fetch Kitty.

As Kitty strolled through the door, I raised one of my feet and exclaimed, "Look, Kitty Cat! My big toe is festering! It may need to be amputated! Do you think you could call your mom and ask about it?"

Stifling what appeared to be a laugh, Kitty took one look at my big toe blister and proclaimed, "It's nothing, you little kook. Get up and quit being such a baby."

"OUT!" I cried. I was very glad I hadn't paid good money for that diagnosis. "Send Bonita and Lulu in!" I quite reluctantly added, "Please."

Bonita and Lulu came in together, barely glanced at my toe, and started cackling like loons! That did it! If all these girls were going to make fun of my debilitating sports injury, then I didn't want them lollygagging around me. What did any of them know about medicine anyway? Not one of them carried around Iodine and bandages like I did!

Since I didn't want word of my dire medical condition to get out and ruin everyone else's fun ---- I knew how they'd worry ---- I told the girls to keep the news of my blister, soon to be BLOOD blister, to themselves. Then I sadly confided that I needed time to myself to adjust to my new physical circumstances. Without batting a single eyelash between them, Bonita and Lulu hollered, "Bye,

Gooney Bird!" and ran out the door, leaving me to console myself.

I remained in the bathroom alone, trying to make sense out of all that had happened to my toe. A few girls came and went, but upon witnessing me in my pathetic state, they'd hightail it out as fast as their roller skates would take them. Not wanting to spread misery around the roller rink, I decided I'd remain in that stinky room, alone, until I could once again emerge as the devil-may-care, always optimistic kid that everyone knew, admired and, yes, revered. After about an hour, I put my socks back on (not the skates!) and hobbled back out to the rink. To my astonishment, no one was there! Only the doofus behind the counter! When I asked where everyone else had gone, he stared blankly at me, slowly rolled his eyes up to the ceiling, shrugged his scrawny shoulders, then mumbled, "They left."

Great! How was I to get back to Purdy? I asked Mr. Goofball if I could borrow a pair of skates so I could skate back to Purdy. He stared blankly at me, slowly rolled his eyes up to the ceiling, shrugged his scrawny shoulders, then . . . OH, FORGET IT! A taxi was out of the question since all I had on me was my pink beach bag containing a half-eaten bag of Fritos and my first aid kit supplied with Iodine and bandages. There was only one option left that I could think of, so out I went to stand in front of the roller skating rink, my thumb pointing toward Purdy ---- well, what I THOUGHT was Purdy.

In only a couple of minutes, to my great delight, a car approached that looked vaguely familiar. It came rather slowly at first, sped up when it went past me, then abruptly slammed to a halt. I ran as fast as I could to catch up with it, then cautiously peered in the open window to make sure there wasn't a creepy serial killer in there. There wasn't, as luck would have it, and who did I see looking straight back at me? Cheery Perkins, that's who! Another stroke of luck! I then glanced over at the driver and when I heard the words, "YOU again!" I knew immediately who it was.

"Hi, Gil," I said sweetly, plastering the biggest smile on my mug I could possibly muster.

"Get in the back!" he snapped. Once again. Backseat. You'd think I had cooties or something. Well, beggars can't be choosers, so . . .

On the drive back to Purdy, I recounted the devastating tale of my big toe blood blister. Yes, it did turn into a blood blister, just as I'd so wisely predicted; however I did not put any Iodine on it. That stuff hurts like the dickens! During the telling of my story, Gil seemed to be holding back a rude chuckle but Cheery made the appropriate utterances of sympathy, as any normal person would. All the way home I chattered about the wonderful day I'd had, with the exception of the toe injury and Mr. Pitman's silly collapse. A couple of times Cheery acted as if she wanted to say something but she was too slow in getting it out, so I forged ahead. Gil never made any contribution to the conversation, other than to snort occasionally.

Arriving back at our hometown, Gil was all set to deposit me on the outskirts of town near the Purdy Football Field, but Cheery sweet-talked him into driving me all the way home. After thanking Gil profusely, to which he nodded once then muttered, "Get out," I finally walked into my house, several hours later than was anticipated. I was in big trouble; Mom wanted to know what had made me so late. I very logically explained how it was not at all my fault. I determined the fault lay with one, or all, of three people: #1 - Mr. Peabody, for making me skate in those circles; B - Mr. Goofball, for giving me rotten skates; #3 - Gil, for not driving faster. My mom had her own idea about who was to blame, but it was so ridiculous I won't even bother to write it down.

# FUN AT
# THE NECKIN DRIVE-IN

One of the neatest things to do on a Friday or Saturday night in Purdy was to go to the Neckin Drive-In, a family-owned hangout run by Homer Neckin and his many offspring. It was closed during the winter months, but in the summertime it was packed with old jalopies brimming with teenagers, especially on the special nights when admission was determined by the car, not the number of people in the car. When each person in the car had to buy a ticket, frugal risk takers would often hide in the trunk to avoid paying the quarter. I never considered this to be a good option for myself, since I feared being forgotten and left to rot, until the car was eventually sold to a new owner.

As with every other high school girl I knew, I didn't own a car and my parents refused to let me take the '49 Chevy to the drive-in. I never really minded not having one, unless there was a movie I just had to see. Such was the case when Tammy and the Bachelor came to town. I absolutely worshipped Debbie Reynolds and if I couldn't see that movie, I would positively DIE! Not only was Debbie the most beautiful starlet in Hollywood, but she was the best singer, dancer and actress to boot! Well, I racked my brain trying to think of a way to get into that movie. A lot of ---- well, to be more precise ---- ALL of my friends refused to take me with them, citing my tendency to continuously explain the plot as the film rolled along. Who could I go with? Finally I came up with a brainstorm: I could go with Gil Snedley and his girlfriend, Cheery Perkins, two of the biggest movie buffs I knew!

In my most genteel voice, laced with the courteous and correct "may" instead of "can," I earnestly pleaded my case: "Cheery, may I please ride with you and Gil to see Tammy and the Bachelor Friday night? I know you're going, because you guys go every Friday and Saturday night, even when the movies are the same both nights, which makes no sense to me whatsoever, but anyway --- puuleese may I go with you?" I attempted to squeeze a couple of tears from my emerald green eyes.

Cheery frowned, in a rather unattractive way, and snottily replied, "No, Trixie, I don't think so. We like to be alone."

Alone? What for? There was plenty of room for me in that clunker! Changing tactics, I rebounded, "Well, Cheery, it seems to me you owe me big time for doing you that favor a couple of weeks ago when you were in dire straits."

Pondering my threat, she glared at me, then said, "Oh, you mean that time you let me copy your geometry homework, because I'd been out with Gil the night before and hadn't done mine? THAT time? The time I got my one and only "F" in geometry because all the answers ---- YOUR answers ---- were wrong?"

I cleared my throat slightly, then sweetly replied, "Yes, Cheery, that time. Did I give you any guarantee about the correctness of those answers? I don't THINK so." Then, toughening my stance, I added, "So, here's the deal, kiddo. Either I go with you and Gil Friday night or I rat you out to Pop McNultie. He's the crabbiest teacher at PHS and he won't like you cheating one teensy-weensy bit. I'll simply explain that you stole my paper."

Okay, that was dirty, I know. And I did feel a twinge of guilt ---- but remember, I was positively desperate to see Tammy! The Cheery and Gil duo was my only hope of going!

Defeated and fully aware of that giant barrel over which I had her, Cheery reluctantly agreed to let me ride along.

Hot diggity dog! The three of us were going to the Neckin Drive-In Friday night! I thanked Cheery profusely, however she merely stuck out her tongue at me, turned on her heel, and strode off. I don't know what she was so mad about. I told her I'd gladly sit in the back, instead of in the middle ---- up front ---- where I really wanted to.

The long-anticipated night finally arrived and the three of us were settling in to enjoy the previews, when

Gil unexpectedly tossed me a quarter. "Here, Trixie. Why don't you SLOWLY walk on over to the concession stand and buy yourself some popcorn and Milk Duds? Assuming you can find the concession stand, which is iffy. Oh, and eat that stuff there. I don't want any junk in my car."

Gee! What a swell guy! A free ride AND free food! I climbed out of the backseat and headed toward the concession stand, which was located in the middle of the drive-in. Any lame-brained dimwit could have found it, Gil! Along the way I stopped to peek into some of the cars and noticed something very goofy. Instead of sitting up front, like normal people, all these kids I knew from Purdy High were lollygagging in the back seat. I didn't understand how they could possibly view the movie, let alone eat any popcorn, considering the dumb way they were reclined. Boy, was it ever hard to see in, what with all that fog on the windows! I plastered my face on the glass, and cupped my eyes to get a good look and say hi, but all I got in return were several nasty "get lost" and a flurry of bad words.

Humph! Fine! If they wanted to waste their money like that, it was no skin off my nose. (Speaking of which, I did scrape off a little nose skin, trying to see through those foggy windows.) But come Monday, when they had no idea how the movie had ended, they'd better not come crying to me!

I proceeded to the concession stand, which I managed to find all by myself, and scarfed down my snacks as fast as I could. Making it back to the car in precisely eleven minutes, I realized the previews were over. As I jumped in the backseat, Gil turned around and snapped, "YOU again? Here, take another quarter and go eat some more popcorn! And stay there until you've eaten every kernel!"

Well, never one to say no to anything free, I marched back to the stand for more popcorn, but this time I added a few licorice sticks and a cherry Coke. It took me a little longer to eat everything this go round, but I still managed to make it back to the car in under twenty minutes - seventeen minutes, to be exact. Gil took one look at me, rolled his eyes, removed his arm from around Cheery's shoulders, then growled between clenched teeth, "Oh heck (he used the word that rhymes with "bell"), we might as well watch this stupid movie."

Stupid?! Stupid?! Yes! Gil called Tammy and the Bachelor stupid! Oh, I couldn't believe my ears! I was so upset I began heaving uncontrollably and throwing up all over the back seat. Nerves ---- plus two large boxes of popcorn, one box of Milk Duds, six licorice sticks, and one cherry Coke ---- will do that to me. Luckily for Gil, there was a big empty Coke cup lying outside the car, so I was able to catch a lot of it.

As my puking subsided, I became acutely aware of Gil's state of mind: he was pretty steamed. The rattled guy ranted and raved for about half an hour, all the while opening and closing the doors to "air out" his precious clunker. Extremely inconsiderate, I thought. Because of all that ranting and raving and opening and closing, I'd missed the first smooching scene between Tammy and Peter! Plus, I'D been the one upchucking like a firehose, not him! Honestly, Gil should stop thinking of himself so much. And was it necessary for Cheery to keep patting his arm, as if he were a scolded puppy? At last, forcing himself to gain control of his nonsensical emotions, Gil looked me straight in my emerald green eyes and hissed, "Trixie, you have two choices." He kept balling and unballing his fists, which unnerved me a little. Then he continued in a hushed, strained voice, as I sat as still as an Egyptian mummy. "You can either watch the rest of the movie standing outside the car with your ear to the speaker, or I will drive you home right this very instant."

Whew! Is that all? Of course I wouldn't mind standing outside! I would do anything to watch the rest of my favorite movie! And, frankly, standing by the car for a couple of hours wasn't all that bad. It afforded me an excellent opportunity to holler at my friends as they walked by. The only drawback was when it started to rain. Unfortunately, the only thing I had for an umbrella was an extra large popcorn bucket, which worked quite well as a rain cap, but which provoked a bunch of mean people behind me to yell, "Get your big, fat, stupid bucket-head out of the way, you dunce!" Or something along those lines. Some things are best forgotten.

When the best movie ever to have been made in the history of Hollywood was finally over, Gil let me back in the car. Actually,I hadn't realized until then he'd locked me out All the way to my house, I kept chattering about how wonderful the movie was, especially with that fabulous surprise ending!

"Wasn't it neat the way Tammy and Peter got together in the end? Wasn't it romantic the way they kissed? Wasn't it swell the way Leslie Nielsen asked Debbie Reynolds to marry him?"

I was utterly overwhelmed by the depth of it all. I could barely contain my euphoria, until the moment we reached my house. Then, like a bolt of divine inspiration, it came to me! I knew what I had to do. I leaned over the front seat, poked my head in between the two lovebirds, and exclaimed, "Hey, Gil! I've got a terrific idea! Why don't you propose to Cheery the way Peter proposed to Tammy?"

For a split second, Gil looked a trifle taken aback, but then, as he slowly tilted his handsome head and flashed that cool, cowboy grin of his, Gil turned to his beautiful beloved and asked, "Whaddya think, Cheery? Want to?"

Well, I don't have to tell you what Cheery's answer was! Those two hugged and kissed just like they hadn't seen each other in a coon's age! I finally had to clear my throat to remind them I was in the back seat. I thanked them for taking me to the drive-in, as well as the Christmas Hop one year, and for chauffeuring me back home to Purdy from Slippery Rock on senior ditch day. I quietly got out of the car and gently waved as they took off. As I watched them drive away, I wistfully thought to myself, "I hope these upcoming nuptials won't affect our future threesomes."

# THE 1915 PHS REUNION

When I was a senior at good ol' Purdy High in 1965, I had the most important job in the school: Feature Editor of The Squirrely Times, the school newspaper. Our journalism teacher was an easy-going, former newspaperman by the name of Mr. Nikniewicz. Since his moniker was rather complicated, requiring a mouthful of unusual letter combinations, everyone agreed he would simply be called Mr. Nick. If, for some strange reason, you did need to remember how to spell his full last name, there was an easy trick to it. Just sing it to the Mickey Mouse song: NIK - NIE - WICZ.

One fine day Mr. Nick came to me with an assignment. It seemed the PHS class of 1915 was going to be celebrating its 50th reunion in the school cafeteria. I was to attend this conglomeration of old-timers and subsequently write an article about it for The Squirrely Times.

Well, to be perfectly honest, I wasn't very gung-ho about doing this because I had a multitude of worries surrounding the whole business ---- worries that people with far less awareness than yours truly would not have. But I, being as astute as is humanly possible, was able to foresee inevitable calamities.

The first major problem I envisioned had to do with the 6'5", 120-pound senior, Barney Flume, whose voice had yet to change. Barney had somehow managed to weasel his way onto the staff of The Squirrely Times and proclaim himself photographer. I think Mr. Nick let him get away with this because Barney was always willing to go to any event, no matter the weather conditions, and snap photos right and left. He wasn't very good --- chopping off people's heads or cutting out half the Squirrelettes in the yearbook photo --- but he could be relied on to at least be there and take the mug shots. However, the thing about Barney that disturbed me, especially considering the decrepit souls we were about to mingle with, was his . . . how shall I put this . . . sadistic side.

Barney liked to sneak up on people when they least expected it, with their eyes bulging wide open. He'd then hop to within an inch of his victims' faces and flash the bulb directly in their peepers! Most unsuspecting prey were so surprised they didn't know what had happened. They'd begin shrieking, "I can't see! I can't see!" Barney, the sadistic ninny that he was, would be bent over, laughing hysterically, and squealing "Gotcha!" in that high-pitched, nasally noise of his.

Well, that type of shock to the system might be

tolerable for us hearty high school kids, but how would the pathetic oldsters in their sixties be able to cope with it? Not only would we be blinding a slew of innocent human beings, but we could be placing the school smack dab in the middle of a law suit, if all those geezers decided to sue on account of their temporary affliction. I tell you, I was worried sick!

Another dread for me, and I will admit this was a bit selfish on my part, would be the inability of the fogies to hear my interview questions. I'd read somewhere that people over the age of thirty experience a severe loss of hearing. If that were true, how would the 1915 graduates be able to hear my intelligent questions? Well, they wouldn't! Not without the aide of a bullhorn or rolled up newspaper! I suppose I could have borrowed one of Margie Sweetum's megaphones that had the giant letters "PHS" on the side, but how unprofessional would that look? Me, a reputable newspaper girl, holding a dumb megaphone in my left hand, while trying to take copious notes with my right! Ridiculous! I'd be the laughingstock of the entire pencil-pushing community! Besides, Purdy High's perky head cheerleader, Margie, had already informed me I couldn't borrow her prized megaphone --- something about me losing every single thing she'd ever loaned me. Humph!

Next worry: the size of the school cafeteria. Was it really going to be big enough to hold all the former graduates? I'd heard there were only going to be about twenty attendees, which wasn't bad, but what about the wheelchairs they most certainly would be cruising around in? Those things take up a lot of room! I sincerely felt the entire shebang would be better off if moved outside to the football field, barring a torrential downpour, of course. That way everyone would be free to roam, pop wheelies, or do whatever else they could muster. And, quite importantly, there would be no fret over scratched up walls or dented cafeteria tables.

Speaking of cafeteria tables, what were the old-timers going to have for refreshments? You know most of them, if any, didn't have their own choppers anymore, so what would the chow consist of? The only suitable types of grub I could come up with were Jello (undoubtedly lime), applesauce, and tapioca pudding. I was positive that nuts, hard candies and ice cubes for their prune juice would be out of the question. It was a terrible concern for me, thinking about what would happen if some careless organizer accidentally laid down pecans or sourballs! I could see it all now --- chipped teeth flying from here to kingdom come!

My final gigantic misgiving had to do with the time of the reunion. It was going to be Saturday from one to four in the afternoon. That was all well and good for young people around my age, but what about ancient people over sixty? You KNOW they have to take naps! This reunion was coming right in the middle of their precious siestas! Naturally I was aware they could most likely survive without a nap; that wasn't my worry. It was the fact that they'd get so crabby! Lack of sleep can cause all kinds of irritability problems, especially for old people and babies. If some of these fuddy-duddies didn't become downright cranky, then they'd probably simply drop their heads and fall fast asleep right where they were. I only hoped they wouldn't be anywhere near the Jello bowl.

Oh, I could hardly contain myself, what with all the anguish swirling around inside my head, but Mr. Nick didn't seem to care one teensy-weensy iota! When I approached him and began voicing my concerns, he abruptly cut me off, saying something mean like, "There you go - being Trixie again! Now knock it off and get back to pasting copy!" Sometimes he could be very heartless.

Having no other choice in the matter, I came to the awful conclusion that I was stuck with this worrisome reunion assignment. Barney Flume wanted me to pick him up at his house, which was okay by me since I liked to show off my driving skills, but I gave him some strict instructions before he even got in my '49 Chevy. Getting out of my car and looking way up into his bony face, here's exactly what I said: "Barney Flume, now you listen and listen good! I will have none of your flashbulb nonsense! Do you hear me? Here's how you're going to take pictures today."

I stopped to glare at him for a full thirty seconds, just to make sure he was paying attention, then I continued, "When you get ready to take a picture, you're going to tell everyone that you'll count to four --- one, two, three --- but on the count of four, they're all to shut their eyes good and tight and not open them again until they've waited at least five minutes! Do you get that, Barney? Then you'll take the picture on FOUR, while everyone's eyes are safely closed! Is that perfectly clear, MISTER Flume?"

When he slowly nodded his head up and down, I said, "Okay, repeat it back to me."

He managed to repeat it back verbatim, so I knew he understood the words, but just to be on the safe side and to prevent that sadistic tendency from rearing its ugly head, I plodded ahead in what some might call a nasty, maternal tone: "And if you don't do exactly what I've told you to do, I will find you, wherever you may try to hide, yank you towards me by your giraffe-like tongue, wrap it all the way around your neck,, then rip it out with my bare hands!" With that I wiped my brow, told a speechless Barney to get in the car, and we headed to the reunion.

Thanks to my expert driving, we made it to the reunion way ahead of time. Since I wanted to help wheel everyone around, I'd also asked my two best friends, Margie and Bonita, to meet us at the cafeteria, in case we needed assistance with that. Oddly enough, as it turned out, not one person needed any kind of help getting around . . . that was unexpected, great news! What wasn't great news was the way they all looked. Gee, did they look old! Well, of course they WERE old, so I don't know why I was so surprised, but still, I didn't expect anything quite like this.

I knew my parents were old --- around forty, I believe --- but they didn't look nearly as bad as these poor fossils.

The men were half bald and what little hair they did have was practically all gray. I don't have anything against gray hair, mind you; I was just astonished that nobody had coal black hair like the old Hollywood stars I'd see on the movie screen. And the same hair thing with the women - gray, white and sometimes even blue, which, truth be told, I found rather fetching. My P.E. teacher, Miss Corey, also had that azure hue on her hair. I liked it so much, I was thinking of dyeing my own hair that bold, sapphire color, if my mom would let me.

What I wasn't crazy about were all those lines in their faces, wrinkles they're called. I guess somebody thought "wrinkle" was a much cuter word than "rut" and decided to call them that. I agree; it is cuter. I don't know what they'd done to create such disfiguring crevices in their mugs, but I sure didn't want it to happen to me! I planned on doing research into that horrible problem, just as soon as I could get my mitts on an Encyclopedia Britannica. I'd heard the expression "as wrinkled as prunes" and now, sadly, I knew precisely what it meant. Of course I had nothing against prunes, personally, as I knew for a fact they were good for certain "digestive issues" --- especially for oldsters over twenty-five.

While I was observing the long-in-the-tooth graduates, as they encountered each other for the first time in a coon's age, I was struck by how friendly they were to each other.

They were positively giddy! Hugging and slobbering all over each other, just like French people! They didn't seem to notice how old, lined and liver-spotted they looked; in fact, they were telling each other how swell they looked. I even overheard them telling each other one of the biggest whoppers I'd ever heard in my entire life --- that they hadn't changed a bit in fifty years! Holy cow! When I heard that, all I could think of was, boy howdy, they must have looked horrible as football players and pom-pom girls! Oh well, my parents always taught me beauty is only skin deep and don't judge a book by its cover and it's what's inside that counts, so I valiantly tried to overlook their shiny pates, saggy skin, and liver spots as I courageously forged ahead with my interviews.

I tentatively wandered around the cafeteria until my eyes landed on a smiling, burly man who looked like he wouldn't mind baring his soul to a gifted writer. This gentleman's name was Mr. McCrackle and he seemed thrilled at the thought of having his name appear in The Squirrely Times. Well, who wouldn't?

"So, Mr. McCrackle," I began, "I drive a '49 Chevy. It's not really mine; it's my parents', but they let me drive it on special occasions, like today. Sometimes we jokingly refer to it as the Sherman tank because it's so sturdy. It's kind of gray with dark blue trim. What kind of car did you drive to school?" I thought this would be a suitable introductory question to break the ice, so to speak.

"Drive a CAR to school? We didn't have any cars to drive

to school, Little Lady! We either walked or rode a horse! Sometimes we'd walk five miles to and fro in one day!"

Wow! Quite an imagination for an old gent! Barreling ahead I said, "Well, if you didn't have a car, Mr. McCrackle, I guess you didn't get to go to the drive-in very often to see neat shows like Tammy and the Bachelor or Dracula."

"Drive-ins and color movies? Little Lady, haven't you ever taken a history class? There were no drive-ins and what few movies we had were in black and white and, to top it off, there were no spoken words, just writing at the bottom of the screen. And sometimes a person would play the piano in front of the stage for background music."

Oh, good grief. Now Mr. McCrackle was sounding senile. Taking a deep breath and forcing myself to be patient and ask another question, I inquired, "Mr. McCrackle, did you do the Twist as a teenager? I'm pretty good at it myself; in fact I was thinking of entering the Miss Yippee County beauty contest and doing the Twist for the talent portion. What do you think about that?"

Mr. McCrackle seemed a little perplexed by the question --- I don't know why; it seemed like a perfectly sane question to me --- but he attempted to answer anyway. "Well, Little Lady, I'll tell you what. I think you should do whatever you think you should. Don't set any limits on yourself. Life's too short. When you have a dream, you should go for it."

Okay, well that was a good answer, I guess, so maybe I was wrong about that senile bit. I decided it was safe to ask another question. "So, if you didn't do the Twist, which I'm given to believe you didn't, considering that evasive answer of yours, what kind of dances did you do?"

"We lived our teenage years during the Era of Ragtime," he replied. "Do you know about that, Little Lady?"

Oh, brother! I wasn't about to let myself get sucked into one of his poppycock statements again, so I mentally told myself it was time to end this looney interview. Thanking the very friendly, but obviously demented, Mr. McCrackle, I wished him a happy reunion, then thought it best to move on.

Spotting a table surrounded by old gents, I proceeded to plunk myself down in an empty chair. I was doing my best to blurt out questions, but it was nearly impossible to hear. They were chortling and yakking at each other so noisily that I couldn't get a word in edge-wise. If, by some miracle, I did manage to ask a question, some gussied-up gal would come along and ask the man to dance, brazenly interrupting me. Then the two of them would stroll onto the dance floor and begin bobbing around, doing something they called the Charleston, a goofy dance that had none of the refinement of our Twist. Every single time I asked one of the gentlemen a very important question, he'd mutter, "Uh-huh" while turning his head to blabber to some former classmate. Quite frankly, my interviews were going nowhere and it was becoming perturbing the way they all ignored me and preferred to chatter and dance with their old cronies.

At this point I figured maybe a member of the fairer sex would be more likely to have her wits about her and be willing to answer a few questions. Scanning the cafeteria, I latched onto a little-bitty, white-haired cutie pie named Mrs. Peacock. Her name was quite befitting, as her frock was an array of lavenders, blues and pinks. I proceeded to question Mrs. Peacock in the same manner as I had Mr. McCrackle, but regrettably she began spouting the same baloney as Mr. Mac. I wasn't sure if they'd conspired to make me look foolish with all that hooey or if they truly believed what they were saying. Either way I knew I couldn't continue with the interviews. I had my impeccable journalistic integrity to consider, just like Mr. Walter Cronkite, the revered news reporter. You simply cannot, as a reputable writer, go around making up fanciful stories just to sell a few papers. I closed my notebook, waved adieu to the elders, and told my crew we were hitting the road.

Standing by our cars to go home, Margie, Bonita and Barney asked if I'd like to meet up with them at the Gulp n Gobble. Barney had decided he wanted to ride with them since he had a huge crush on Margie, which everybody in the school knew about --- except Barney. I told them I had to get home, grab my transistor radio and hightail it over to my job at La Belle Beauty Shop.

As I was driving home by myself, I thought about what my new friends had told me --- about how Purdy had been, and still was, one of the greatest little towns in the world. I drove by the Moose Theater, the Purdy

Bowling Lanes and continued down Curley Street; I parked in front of the Yippee County Courthouse, admiring its classic gazebo and fountain; I proceeded along the narrow tree-lined streets to my house on Fairgrounds Avenue, a home that would be incomplete without my parents and Queenie; I gazed toward the "P" Mountain, which had come to symbolize all my memories of Purdy. I was seeing the town anew through the eyes of much older people, people who'd spent nearly seventy years of their lives in the town. They'd unequivocally declared that Purdy had been the most wonderful place in which to grow up, raise their families, and grow old. I didn't know about all of that yet, but I did suddenly realize what an amazing town I'd been lucky enough to grow up in and what an incredible high school I'd been fortunate enough to be a part of. Blinking back tears, I whispered, "Thank you, Purdy. And thank you, Purdy High."

Printed in the United States
By Bookmasters